SAE It Isn't So

PATRICK B. MURPHY

To Nancy, Reed, and Grant
who listened to this book for years

Chapter 1 – January 28 - Danny

What if you were a Quaker? The thought ran through my mind as the wind ran through my hair. You would be a pacifist and very reflective. Which could come in handy while walking along a dark country road at night. Just like this road to the Quaker Durham Friends School. I drive this road five days a week to teach Spanish, but I've never walked it at night.

I parked my '83 Spider next to the stairway that led to the High School and my classroom. My beat up Spider blended well with the weathered wooden building and the lob lolly pines. I walked through the school and into my office. Just like in a noir detective movie, I made my own coffee and ate a doughnut at my desk. I logged into the network and was greeted by five messages from parents and about fifty more messages from the recent email virus attack that hit the school. The DFS network had been down for three days last week. I was collecting the offending emails to help diagnose what had happened.

It is my habit to unplug my desk phone so I wasn't surprised to hear the PA system blare "Mr. Danny Yobar, please come to the administration building." I prepped my coffee to go and started whistling 'Violets for your Furs'. Maybe they wanted to give me a raise.

I walked a short ways through a thin stand of pines to the administration building. I took all three steps at once into the building's open door because I could. Mrs. Carson was at the coffee machine as I came in.

We exchanged greetings but I could tell she was perturbed that I was both late and unreachable by phone. I gave her a look that said I would try to be better next time.

Maybe.

I smiled and sat down on a metal chair with an old gray leather seat just outside the principal's office. Despite what Ms. Carson may wish, I knew that Principal Nygren wouldn't call me down here to chastise my tardiness; he wanted me to help with the computer system again. So while I waited five minutes, I drank my coffee and finally Dr.

Nygren emerged from his office and invited me in. I put my empty coffee cup on Mrs. Carson's table.

My wait has a cost.

I was happy enough to help fix the network. It was fun and I have learned enough Internet lingo to perplex my dad. The school's network was 'managed' by the son of the biggest donor to the school. And the school needs big donors to pay for teachers' sports cars—so Dr. Nygren had repeatedly told me. I was glad that *someone* considered my dilapidated Spider a sports car.

Dr. Nygren met me at his door with a paternal smile and a soft handshake. "Buenas dias, Danny. How are you today?" His mild voice matched his fatherly visage. His silver-white hair, with a few wisps of brown still battling, was combed neatly over his forehead. A nondescript shirt went well with his brown slacks and brown shoes.

"I'm doing fine. But it's 'buen*os*' dias, not 'buen*as*' dias ."

I can be a stickler when I want to be.

We went into his office and sat down. His gray desk was covered with neat piles of papers, travel mementos, and pictures of his family. The one perk of principality that he indulged in was custom built bookshelves. The room was lined with bookshelves built into all the walls, the only exception being the window facing into the woods. A birdfeeder hung from the bough that was framed in the window.

"Danny, I'd like you to take a look into the network problems we're having, if you don't mind. Things aren't going well and the..... current staff ..... needs help", he started.

Ted was the aforementioned 'current staff', the son of the largest donor to Durham Friends School. Nepotism. 'Nepotisma', in Spanish, but the same result.

'Network problems' was not good news for the over one hundred network connections spread throughout eight DFS school buildings. Our main network server was five years old (time for a new one) and it handled the email system, all user files, and most recently, the web server - which turned out to be a bad idea. The Internet community (not a community of 'Friends' as the Quakers were discovering) had access to our main server after hacking through the 'security' that Ted installed.

I nodded and said, "Did Ted say what the problem was?"

See how well I played together?

"He doesn't know exactly. We still get attacked whenever he reboots the system. Ted doesn't know why, but he's working on it." Dr. Nygren was willing to give Ted the benefit of the doubt for the donor's sake, but I wasn't.

"I can help if I get the system god password." The god password would give me total control of the network. The last time I tried to help solve a problem like this, Ted wouldn't give me the password. But I won't help unless this time unless I get it.

The principal smiled. "OK. I'll get him to give you the password." That essentially ended our meeting.

A few minutes later, I left his office, refilled my empty coffee cup, and sat down again in Mrs. Carson's visitor chair. My next class wasn't for another half hour. I leafed through the Raleigh News and Observer while she worked at her computer. After a few minutes, I picked up my cup and started to leave.

She said without looking up from her computer. "Good thing you didn't leave that dirty cup on my desk again, like you did last week. It was growing things after a few days."

"Ciao, Mrs. Carson." I smiled and walked out into the quad towards my classroom.

I'd be able to fix the Internet problem in a few hours. All I'd have to do is reinstall the operating system, apply a few patches, and juice the firewall. Then I'd have full access to the school web server which would be a lot of fun.

Not that I'm a geek.

Chapter 2 - February 2

Research Triangle Park, North Carolina, was booming. In 1955, the main use of land here was to cover clay – thick clay that made even tobacco farming impossible. Over the next half century, RTP had transformed from sprawling countryside to urban sprawl, modern style. Biotechnology, software development, and pharmaceutical research had replaced lob lolly pines, tractors, and barns. Real estate was so expensive in the prestigious Triangle that newer companies built offices just outside the Park but used PO boxes in RTP as their address. Office buildings sprang up like nandinas unchecked by bush-hogs.

Morrisville, adjacent to RTP, had spawned many such office buildings. At the biotech park located off the I-40 east exit was one of the most recent examples. The red brick building was three stories of nicely rounded corners. There was even a Starbucks in the lobby.

On the third floor were the offices of a clinical monitoring startup company in business for three years. In the kitchen that doubled as a break room, all eight employees were eating the celebratory birthday breakfast for Alexandria Knott, the president of WDM, Inc. ('We Do Monitoring').

Alexandria lifted her dixie cup of orange juice to the crowd and said, "Thank you again for a wonderful birthday party." Alexandria's second in command, Diana Virbius, made one last toast. "Happy thirty fifth!" Diana's almond shaped eyes sparkled and her dark cocoa skin glowed as she smiled. The employees each grabbed one more bagel, refilled their juice, and headed to their offices amid chatter. Alexandria followed Diana to her corner office.

Diana sat down behind her desk, which faced the door. She unconsciously patted down the short curls on her head. Diana's pet hamster spun the wheel with zeal in the glass walled terrarium. Alexandria sat across from her and balanced her bagel plate on her knee.

Alexandria quietly stared at the framed prints of 'The Big Five' animals of Africa. So Diana broke the ice.

"Big meeting with the pharma big shots Thursday, huh? If we get the contract, you make the company. But no pressure." Diana reflexively pulled her unbuttoned sweater across her chest, but very, very slowly it opened again. The hamster made the ball bearing dance in the water tube.

Alexandria carefully considered spilling the remains of her dixie cup orange juice on the new carpet in revenge. A good retort to the joke but, at the end of the day, Alexandria paid the rent. And the maintenance costs.

"You'll go from 'Senior Clinical Research Associate' to 'Vice President of Clinical Monitoring', is what will happen to you," Alexandria predicted. "And then you'll see how hurtful it is to have your employees make fun of you on your birthday."

Diana Virbius was thirty one years old and had been a clinical monitor for five years. She was just getting used to the 'Senior' appellation. After graduating from NC State University with a double major in forestry and Latin, she followed up with a Clinical Research Associate certificate from State. She was still young enough to think that 'Vice President' sounded like a good thing. Under her window the sun glowed on her silver Honda Accord. It could soon be a Lexus if they won this contract. A certified pre-owned Lexus, but a Lexus.

Diana turned her gaze back to her boss. Alexandria was pressing buttons on her smart phone, the newest on the

market. "All the CEOs have one! It's even got Bluetooth!",
Alexandria had said with a funny voice when she first got it.

It was hard to read Alexandria's blue eyes. Alexandria
exuded competence and confidence. Diana believed. Trust,
but verify. "So what's your plan for the meeting?"

Alexandria finished chewing a small but tenacious bite of
bagel before answering. "We're having dinner at The White
Elephant, that Thai-Indian place in Durham. Arthur Moore,
of course, will be there. And he said he's bringing his
director of clinical trials to meet me." She took a small sip of
the unspilled juice. Her signature red lipstick recorded the
event on the cup.

"I gave them the proposal, budget, and presentation last
week. We've talked a few times since. I'll find out Thursday
if we win but I'm worried about this clinical trials guy. He'll
probably be the principal investigator for the trial. If I don't
make a good impression, who knows what he'll decide."

Diana smiled and replied, "What's not to like? You're a tall,
gorgeous blond woman. He'll probably be looking for a way
to give you the contract just so he can check you out at the
monthly meetings."

Alexandria gave a small laugh and straightened up
automatically. "The blond is getting a few streaks of gray

that need hiding. My old jeans don't fit quite as well either. But it's nice of you to say so." Alexandria gave a mock look of surprise. "It's a birthday present!" Diana laughed.

Diana was impressed that her friend Alexandria had started WDM at such great personal financial risk. Alexandria left a lucrative job at Quintiles, the largest clinical research organization in the world, to start this company. Alexandria had always wanted to be more of her own boss and deep down wanted to prove that she could succeed at her own business. Three years in, still in business.

Alexandria's fledgling company had grown to eight people: Alexandria, Diana, three senior clinical research associates with several years experience, two entry level clinical associates, and a receptionist/secretary/administrator. She relied upon a company down the hall to help with the computer network as needed. WDM had only six contracts and needed this new clinical trial from Arthur Moore Pharmaceuticals.

"That PI guy is probably just there to make sure the papers get signed right," Diana offered, seeing the concerned look on her friend's face.

But WDM hadn't succeeded by accident, and certainly not by worrying if some PI was going to like her. Alexandria straightened again in her seat and announced confidently,

"We'll get the contract. We've done HIV vaccine studies before. This Phase I/II project is a little different because it will include subjects at high risk for HIV acquisition in addition to healthy volunteers. I'm an expert, dare I say on my birthday, in safety lab data. I know we were the lowest price. I think I even convinced Arthur Moore that I trusted the Internet." She paused. "That's the weirdest part of this contract. Not the electronic data capture, but that all monitoring and reporting must be electronic – no paper copies. Well, that should make things easier."

By habit, Alexandria reached into her pocket and reapplied her trademark red lipstick. After smacking her lips, Alexandria stood up to her full five feet eight inches, dumped her uneaten bagel in the flowered garbage can (those carbs were eying my hips as a permanent home, she thought), and wiped the crumbs off her bright blue dress.

She told Diana, "If the vaccine shows a good safety profile, no serious adverse events, then I'm sure we'll be the monitors for the follow up efficacy trials. The company will quadruple in size in two years." The back of her neck tingled as she imagined her dreams of success materializing. "Of course, if there are a lot of SAEs, then it's back to the drawing board."

She walked down the hall into her corner office. It was the same size as Diana's, but hers was the CEO's office. It said so right on the door. She slid her tall frame into her computer chair, picking up her coffee cup with one hand and clicking on the Internet icon on her computer with the other. She drank her coffee as she read through, for the tenth time, all the information on the Arthur Moore Pharmaceuticals website.

Chapter 3 - February 5 - Danny

The roof leaked on my Spider, so I was soaked on my left
side by the time I got to my dad's house stoop. While I was
still stomping water off my shoes on the welcome mat, the
door opened and dad poemed, " 'Their scantly leav'd and
finely tapering stems had not yet lost those starry diadems,
Caught from the early sobbing of the morn.' John Keats."
He stepped back and I entered the foyer. "This isn't exactly
dew, Dad." I don't like to encourage him but it does have its
little joys.

My father's house was furnished with art from all over the
world which created a freakishly incoherent decor. The
floors were thick hardwood harvested from a nearby
dilapidated barn. The yellow foyer was decorated with
masks from Mexico, necklaces from Kenya, and feathers
from the Navajo Reservation. Opposite the door to the
hallway bathroom was a tall, tapered, teak table from

Thailand. In its top drawer was a small black lacquer box with a hand painted lid displaying a family of elephants. The box contained small safety pins, fortune cookie papers 'You are social and entertaining' and 'The butterfly is free to fly', a DC Metro pass with a $12.85 balance, coins of dong, baht, yuan, pence, and a small tie clip with a picture of a wave breaking in the Atlantic Ocean.

I swung by the beer storage unit and grabbed a fine specimen, then walked two steps down into the living room and sat on the couch opposite dad's easy chair. Dad was right behind me.

Dad was about five feet ten inches, but he looked shorter because of his face. He had an impressive set of hair. Across his forehead, the thick locks spectrumed from brown to gray to white. Though his hair was relatively short, it fully framed his face. His sideburns mutton-chopped their way down to his jaw line. The final element squeezing out his facial real estate were brushy eyebrows which were not so long but so very thick.

One of his printers in the corner was loudly spewing out about a page a minute. He answered my quizzical glance by saying, "It's for my art junk-email project." My eyebrows raised in mock understanding. My dear old dad was creating junk-email art. I refrained from asking for further details.

I looked through the large window at the back of the house. At this time of year, the view consisted of pine trees and bare oaks. Still, the little forest blocked out the view of the closest neighbor, a thousand feet away. A creek ran through the trees, a meandering channel sometimes dammed by beavers. The beavers left their calling card: all saplings with a diameter of less than one inch were gnawed down to a height of one foot. I can still remember the feel of the cold water rushing through my fingers as I played by this creek as a child. I thought I heard the creek now but it was probably just the printer humming in the corner.

Okay, he had me. "Dad, why in the world are you making a junk-email object d'art? And who exactly has determined that it's art?" I was too stubborn to ask exactly *what* a junk mail art exhibit was. I still have some pride.

My dad eased his lanky frame onto the couch. He favored his right knee as he settled into the corner. I don't think of my dad as getting old, but he is fifty five. A few aches and pains were to be expected, but I still liked to think of him as a young-ish man. He always had been. I am still younger than he was when I was born.

Dad pointed to the "exhibit" and said, "It's art in the guise of data management." His voice was deep and just a little gravely. "This exhibit started with only one type of junk email: emails asking for your checking account to launder large amounts of money. You know, the widow of a deposed general has received an inheritance. But she can only deposit the check in a U.S. bank. Just send her your checking account information, then she'll deposit the check, and you'll get to keep a nice little commission for your troubles."

The printer ran out of paper and dad sprang up (he must have seen me notice him limping before) and added some fresh paper – fancy paper that ran fifty cents a pop. Art ain't cheap. He lowered himself into his chair again and took a swig from his cold Dinkel Acker beer bottle.

"Then the emails started coming from different countries," he started in again. "Then the source of the money started changing: unclaimed bank account from deceased tourists, oil revenue, wedding dowries. My database tracks the countries and the details of the scam. I've tracked the frequency of the swindle by country, by year. It makes for a pretty cool graphic. Then I combine the details of some of the more interesting versions – that's the art."

I guess the look on my face made him press on earnestly. "I'll use the database application and graphs as an example in the RTP clinical data managers users group meeting."

I must have still looked unimpressed. Dad blurted out, "I'm going to sell the results to spam blocker developers so they can use the data to predict the next wave of emails. It's called big data." I finally displayed enough credulity that he relaxed back into his chair.

"Anyway", he concluded.

A perfect time to change the subject. I dove in.

"Dr. Nygren asked me to help fix the DFS network because of this email virus attack the school is under. This time I'll get the god password and I can set things up so even Ted can't screw it up."

Dad's eyes lit up; not as much as when a good pun was brewing, but he loved working on networks and I was hoping he had some new advice for me.

He nodded towards the web server on his desk. We got up and he sat down in the computer's driver chair. His web server was connected to a sweet Cisco firewall that I wasn't sure the school could afford. "I just installed some new freeware," he said. "Actually, I downloaded the professional version and it was $150. But let me show you what it can do."

He logged on to his network by entering a dauntingly long password with numbers, and shifted keys. I'm not good at passwords but dad apparently is.

After a few more clicks, a slick looking report showed up on the screen. He said, "This report shows the IP address of everyone who has accessed the user group website in the past month. I can track it down by page visited even. Look." He clicked on the 'Usage Report' and pointed. "In the last two days, three people from Research Triangle Institute accessed the page. If I really wanted to, I could probably track down the exact users."

He clicked again and showed me another report. "I can drill down by user and find out which pages each user looked at. This would be a great report for you keep track of who is using your web pages and also anyone who might be poking around and crashing your network."

I was impressed. It was definitely cool. "Can you email me the link to the software site? A hundred fifty bucks? It looks worth it." He shot me a quick email with the link and then went back to the window with the monitoring software running. He stood and I took his place in the driver's seat and continued to check out the program.

The rain had slowed to a soft drizzle. Dad walked out the solarium door, stretched his knee, and headed to his chicken pen. Dad had been raising backyard chickens for nearly five years. This year's 'biddies' had just moved from the bathtub to an outdoor enclosed pen with heat lights. The chicken pen was the size of a greenhouse, built of black metal stakes wrapped with chicken wire. He had even made a small door for those chickens. Ten biddies were sporadically peeping, pecking the ground along with fifteen hens ranging from one to two years old. Dad filled their corn containers and water dishes and clucked back at the unimpressed chickens.

I logged off the server, went back to the couch, and picked up dad's copy of James Joyce's *Ulysses* from the coffee table. Dad had marked his favorite passages with dots in the margins. I surfed the book, stopping to read at his dots, marveling at Joyce, and wondering about my father.

When dad came back in, I put down the book, thanked him for the software tip and told him I had to go. He walked me to the door.

"How's that new girlfriend Barbara of yours doing?" he asked.

"Brenda? She's not really my girlfriend. We've just been out a few times." I didn't want to sound snippy but I must have.

"I was just asking," he said with just a little hurt in his voice.

To change the subject before I left, I asked, "Don't you have a pithy quote for me before I go?"

He smiled and said, "Live for one detailed potato not a top deli at Eden or of evil."

"Dad, that doesn't even make sense."

He smiled bigger and said, "At least it makes as much sense backwards as it does forwards."

Chapter 4 - February 5

From bakery, to barbeque shack, to hamburger joint, to Thai Indian cuisine, the building currently housing The White Elephant was prosaic on the outside and poetic on the inside. Warm tones sprang from the walls and floor and ceiling. The gentle peace of Asian decorating wound through the restaurant. After she entered, Alexandria Knott nodded to the hostess with a smile to indicate that she had seen where her party was already seated. She kept the smile on as she approached the table wondering how it was that she was thirty minutes early for the meeting but she was already late. They were sharing an appetizer and drinking beers.

Arthur Moore and Blake Roth stood as she approached them. Moore was a good looking early sixty-ish, Alexandria thought, and a good decision to go with the bald look – not easy for a white guy. He was trim and wearing an authentic

Italian suit that fit him well. She didn't know how to read his piercing blue eyes.

Arthur extended his hand to Alexandria and she shook it. "Alexandria Knott, this is Blake Roth, principal investigator of the HIV vaccine trial and Director of Clinical Trials at AMP." Blake was a solid six feet, mid-thirties, and still retained his boyish good looks. He had fine brown hair and sideburns down just past his ears. His brown eyes locked onto Alexandria's. Blake smiled and waited for his boss to continue.

"Blake, this is Alexandria Knott, CEO of WDM, the clinical monitoring CRO for the trial." Knott and Roth shook hands and exchanged greetings.

Being called 'CEO' usually made Alexandria smile inwardly at the preposterousness (or is it preposteriety?) of the idea. But this time an actual smile did appear because Arthur had said '*the* CRO' instead of '*a* CRO'. Alexandria sat down, and they followed suit.

Arthur smiled and answered her unasked question. "We finished up at the office early so we came here to beat the traffic."

He continued, "I was just getting Blake up to speed on the trial but let me start again." Moore looked very comfortable and very confident as he described his company. "AMP has several products in Phase II and Phase III malaria treatment and prevention clinical trials. We've come up with a new approach for an HIV vaccine based on our malaria vaccines."

Alexandria listened and couldn't help but admire Moore. He was clearly enthusiastic about his company and knew the technical details inside and out. Arthur folded his hands and continued, glancing from time to time between Alexandria and Blake.

"The malaria protection adaptations in blood cells in people from sub-Saharan Africa can be manipulated to make those same cells less susceptible to human immunodeficiency virus I and II", Arthur went on.

"We've engineered a molecule that we think will disrupt HIV insertion into cells better than any other product being tested today. We have completed animal studies and submitted the results to the FDA and we've gotten approval to start a modified Phase I/II safety trial. Most Phase I/II trials only include healthy volunteers, but our request to include high risk volunteers was also approved by the FDA." Moore paused, leaned back, and sipped his beer. A look of excitement had transformed his face during his explanation.

Blake leaned toward Alexandria and said, "When Arthur says 'we' and 'our', he really should be saying 'I' and 'my'. He has been instrumental in the development of the molecule, the conduct of the animal studies, and most importantly, getting support from the venture capitalists."

Blake saw Alexandria's eyes moving over him. His left hand brushed his long hair across his forehead. As he continued to make eye contact with her, he hoped that none of the appetizer was still in his teeth.

"The high risk volunteers include will allow us to make some prevention claims in addition to safety", Blake explained. "This is a big advantage for us. Each trial can be extremely expensive so we want to pick only the best research partners to continue development through clinical trial phases. Currently, ten AMP products are flowing through our R&D life cycle. Our board is resistant to expanding our portfolio; we are at full capacity."

The waitress came by and took Alexandria's order of a glass of red wine. Arthur gave a smile and silent shake of his head to the waitress.

Blake continued earnestly, "This product and this clinical trial are well funded, Ms. Knott, which is rare because it doesn't involve NIH or Gates funding. The National Institutes of Health had their budget cut just like every other federal agency and the Gates Foundation has already allocated their HIV clinical trial budgets for microbicides. There's too many candidates to choose from until one has a successful Phase I/II trial."

"Alex. Please call me Alex." Her smile was more genuine than she had planned.

Blake smiled back and said, "Alex."

Arthur took the baton and continued on-point after a moment of silence as her wine was delivered. "Blake is my best researcher and he will be the principal investigator for the trial. We need to get this product through this safety study to a full blown Phase III efficacy study as soon as possible. To do this, we are going to run this safety trial completely by electronic data capture, including monitoring and reporting. We think we can shave at least two months off the project timeline."

Alexandria knew that the issue of using an EDC system for data management was the weakest part of her proposal to monitor this trial. She was more comfortable with paper records as the original source document but the wave of the future was electronic data capture of source data. She had read about this in the journals for the past five years but it was slow in coming. It made sense in this case, she concluded, because the majority of data for the trial would be pharmacokinetic and safety data delivered electronically from the lab.

But Alexandria also knew that her strength was in her experience monitoring lab data for Phase I trials bound for FDA approval. Phase I trials gather data on the safety and pharmacokinetics of a substance, in this case an HIV vaccine, administered to a small number of volunteers. If the PK shows that the vaccine has a high blood concentration after several weeks without causing serious adverse events, then the vaccine would find more financial backers and progress towards large scale testing in volunteers susceptible to HIV infection. If the high risk volunteers don't acquire HIV during the trial, that is a good indication of the efficacy of the vaccine.

Alexandria sat totally straight, projected her most engaged professional demeanor, and attacked the issue head on.

She spoke directly to Arthur Moore. "I have monitored a few trials with electronic data capture, especially of lab data similar to this trial, but only one in a Phase I/II like this one."

Arthur leaned forward reassuringly. "That won't be a big issue for us, Alex. Your expertise in Good Clinical Practices will be able to get you through the process. By the way, we have a separate bid out to give GCP training to the study staff. Are you interested?"

Almost before she could think not to say it, Alex let out her mantra. "We do monitoring, not GCP training." A quick smile. "WDM – we do monitoring. I'm afraid I've had my fill of GCP training and I'd like my company to focus on monitoring HIV trials."

Arthur continued after a small shrug. "A CEO has to make those kind of decisions." A bonding moment of camaraderie amongst CEO's, Blake thought, but definitely didn't verbalize.

As if an agreement on that point had been reached, Arthur continued, "We have our first site selected, a clinic near Philadelphia, and the site investigator there is great. We need to recruit approximately 300 volunteers at four sites in twelve months. We'll be using the Johns Hopkins lab in Baltimore for the test results. This should make the FDA happy enough to give us approval for a Phase III efficacy trial."

Arthur shifted his six foot frame in his chair and his voice got very excited again. "As I said, we will recruit about 300 participants in twelve months, Alex. We'll need you plus three of your senior clinical research associates to monitor full time for that. And then the Phase III efficacy trial with 2,000 participants." Arthur let that sentence trail off and he could see Alex quickly calculating in her head. This was the break her company needed. Arthur saw the light in her eyes and could almost feel the adrenaline flowing through her.

Arthur glanced at Blake to keep him engaged, then leaned towards Alex with his elbows on the table. "But the first step is this Phase I/II trial. We have venture capital funding to take us through the whole trial – they think we have a chance to have a vaccine before any of the Gates' projects do." The Bill and Melinda Gates Foundation was a big funder of HIV research. Melinda Gates graduated from Duke University and the BMGF has a large presence in the local RTP pharma community.

Arthur pressed on. "The key to a quick submission of the study data is to go completely EDC – all data will be collected electronically. I mean *all* data capture will be electronic. Medical record notes, lab results, protocol deviations, supplies, everything. Well, everything but informed consent. We will still use a paper informed consent form to make the ethics boards happy." He unconsciously smiled condescendingly at the ethics boards in absentia.

"It will be crucial that all data collection, all the monitoring, and all the reporting, Alex, be performed electronically in order to proceed as quickly as possible. Absolutely no paper copies or any copies of study data outside the database system. That will only slow us down."

Arthur waited two beats and then asked the question he had arranged the meeting to ask. "Can you commit to that, Alex?"

Alex locked eyes completely with Arthur but she could feel Blake staring at her. She wasn't comfortable with a completely electronic trial but her experiences with electronic data at least were satisfactory enough. He was asking her to change all her procedures – no paper notes, no information being collected any other way than through the EDC system. As her father told her, success requires risk.

She spoke clearly and without hesitation. "We are totally prepared to meet those requirements. This is an exciting opportunity for us. I'll be the lead monitor and make sure everything goes just the way we want it." Alex felt committed and confident and it sounded so in her steady voice.

Arthur smiled and extended his hand to her. He was in 'good cop' CEO-mode again. "Wonderful, just wonderful Alex. Welcome to the team." She felt his warmth and was convinced that he was genuinely happy that she won the award to monitor the trial. She wanted to continue discussing all the details of the trial.

He looked at his watch and said apologetically, "I'm sorry but I have to leave early. I'm going to head back to the office for a phone call"- Welcome to the team, she thought- "so you and Blake can run through your numbers again and sign the contracts."

They all stood and exchanged good-byes. She sat and tried to come to grips with the fact that the meeting had been a great success.

She heard the sound of his Mercedes revving and accelerating as she took her copy of WDM's proposal out of her briefcase.

Chapter 5 – February 17

It was twenty minutes from the school to Ninth Street in Durham. Ninth Street was one of the main shopping streets near Duke University. The Spider hummed a sweet tune on the short trip through the disappearing country roads until Danny hit Ninth Street. A rare curbside parking spot was available in front of Helena's Bookstore and Danny maneuvered quickly to take it.

The brightly colored sign above Helena's Bookstore had recently been redone in reds and blues. Its handmade uniqueness was a small counterstrike to the mega maul bookstores. But it was the scent of the store that Danny enjoyed. The smell of *The New York Times,* stacks of slowly decaying *Da Vinci Code* hardbacks, and pulp of various sorts perfumed the air. He knew his father would instantly have identified and told him the name of the jazz musician on the CD playing in the store. It was a blessing not to be told.

Danny spotted his mother's henna red hair as she was typing at a computer in the rear of the shop. Danny walked over and peeked at her screen.

"Buying books for the Christmas season?" he asked over her shoulder.

She smiled, turned, and said, "February is a little too early for Christmas books. Books for Summer."

She stood up, put her hands on his shoulders, and gave her son a kiss on the cheek.

"How are you? How is school?" she said while taking her glasses off and finishing off the hug.

Danny sat down in a side chair that belonged to the desk. He put his right hand on the edge of the desk and rubbed the wood admiringly. His mom said she bought it in grad school at UNC from someone who built it as a project for an art class, but Danny had a hard time believing that. It was gorgeous, surely not the work of an evening art class student. Along the back of the desk were pictures of outdoor scenes of nature, mostly from the Eno River which ran through Durham.

"The students are still in shock that Winter break is over. They're still a month or so away from rebellion, so I've got 'em right where I want 'em." Danny stretched, leaned back in his chair, and laced his fingers behind his head.

"Spanish Club is going better this semester. One of the new kids is really into Mexican music so we've got a little band going. That reminds me, when is the Mercedes Nandujar book signing?" His mother recommended Nandujar to him and now she was one of Danny's favorites.

Janice looked at the calendar. "Two Mondays from now, 7:30PM. She just sent me twenty signed books to display."

Danny nodded. He would be here for that one. Maybe extra credit for his Spanish I students.

"How are things going with Brenda?" she asked.

It was still early on in their relationship. The problem with answering questions like these, Danny thought, was that it forced him to crystallize his thoughts despite the fact that it was too early.

"Well, it's just been a few dates, but we've done some really interesting things already. She wanted to go to that prehistoric rock exhibit at the art museum. It was fun and I probably wouldn't have gone without her. So we've got some common interests. Maybe she can come to the Nandujar signing."

He slowly stood up and said his getaway line. "I have to pick up a cake next door so…"

But Janice remembered just as Danny was gaining momentum towards the door.

"Will your band be able to play for the Ninth Street Merchants Association Spring Festival? It's outside this year; it'll be fun, but it's getting late for bookings. I'm already making mistakes as this year's association social director." She stopped. "I really want your quartet but I have to book it by next week."

Danny had put off asking the group about the Ninth Street gig. But she was right, they had to book their gigs in advance as much as possible.

"I'll ask Glenn tonight," Danny said. "Bob and Christina will go along with what he says – they're lost in the bliss of their engagement. He'll be more likely to agree if you also commit to the Christmas Party gig."

Glenn was the leader of their jazz trio/quartet. Danny flexed his hands and wondered if he could still drum after a month and a half of no practice since the intense holiday season.

One thing that Glenn taught him was that a musician could live easy for a few months if you get your holiday gigs lined up right. This had been a busy holiday season.

"Tell Tammy I said hello!" he heard as he left through the front door.

Danny turned left on the side walk and walked a few store fronts down to Renata's, an ice cream store. It felt good to be outside in the cold.

He pushed the glass door open and entered. Renata's was chilly, as most ice cream stores were. He would have to ask Tammy Rose, the owner, why that was – weren't the freezers enough to keep the ice cream cold? The menu on the wall was written with fluorescent chalk. The menu changed each week or so, whenever new flavors rotated through. Today, the specials were Mexican chocolate, almond, lemon sorbet, and German chocolate. The back wall was decorated with knick knacks: a rubber Santa Claus from Europe, a small mahogany statue of a pair of entwined dancers, a tin wind-up toy car.

Tammy was finishing up with a customer so Danny waited and looked around. Tammy placed the customer's change on a hard blue mat with plastic prickles. Danny lowered his eyes as the customer passed him.

"Hey, what's up?" Tammy smiled and said to Danny. Tammy had a friendly full smile that shone beneath her brown eyes, black eyebrows, and short black hair. Danny still considered her older, but she was about thirty five. At five feet three inches, she was about a half foot shorter than Danny.

"Nothing much. Just picking up the cake," he responded.

Tammy walked to the cake case, picked up his cake, and took it to the decorating workspace by the sink.

"I was just displaying it," she said over her shoulder as she filled her pastry writing tool with a thin frosting mix. "I wouldn't have sold it."

She poised the pastry writing bag in her right hand.

"What do you want written on the cake?"

"'Happy Birthday, Mrs. Carson' will do nicely."

When Tammy finished the writing, she angled it towards him for approval. After receiving the nod, she started boxing it. Danny waited patiently for her to ask him to hold down the string with a finger while she made a bow tie knot around the box. But she did not need any help. A true professional.

Danny paid for the cake and for a double espresso to go.

Halfway to the door, he said over his shoulder, "Mom says hi!"

Chapter 6 – February 20

The name of the shopping center was enough to attract Stephen's attention. 'Triangle Square' was at the intersection of NC 54 & NC 55, near the heart of Research Triangle Park. One of the first developments near RTP, it was showing its age but still thrived with restaurants and small family owned businesses. Though one hundred and twenty miles from the nearest beach, a flock of six seagulls rose and fell in the middle of the parking lot, crying out with no waves to listen.

The Savvy Café was located at the western end of the strip mall. An early retirement victim at IBM, Eduardo Tuttlehoff bought the space two years ago, added windows and remodeled it into a large coffee house. The masses in RTP love their coffee, so if it's convenient enough, independent coffee houses can survive even against Starbucks. Stephen and Danny had adopted the Savvy Café as their Friday afternoon coffee meeting venue.

Stephen stood outside the café, watching the seagulls, as Danny's Spider pulled into the parking lot and parked next to the café owner's sweet red Porsche Carrera. Danny got out of the car, hitched up his pants instinctively in preparation for meeting his father, and sauntered up to the sidewalk. Stephen felt the great joy of a father at seeing his grown son wearing a belt, even if it wasn't hitched tightly.

My pants are up, but there's a little more rolling out the top these days, Stephen thought, as he patted his waist.

Danny hopped onto the sidewalk and shook Stephen's hand and they walked through the wooden front door of the café. Danny always thought of it as more of a club than a coffee shop.

The café was dominated by a beautiful wooden reverse L-shaped bar which enclosed the kitchen area and the back left corner of the shop. Three large rectangular mirrors behind the bar were covered with colorful beads and small idols. But the real eye-catcher in the café was the huge mantelpiece covering nearly half the entire right wall. The mantelpiece rose from the wooden floor to the paneled ceiling, festooned with club playbills featuring musicians from around the world. Upon closer review, Danny noticed that four panels comprised the mantle. Each panel was made of dark mahogany and glowed in the sunlight.

Danny's quartet (OK, *Glenn's* quartet) had played here many times. The band would set up in front of the mantelpiece and play their music while the evening coffee drinkers went about their business. At the far back corner on the right, on the way to the restrooms, was one table. A wooden privacy divider blocked the table off from the rest of the café, probably for Eduardo to do paperwork. On the divider, a small sign said in red script on white background 'The Second Room'. There were two chairs and an interesting selection of objects adorning the area. A photo of a European queen was hanging in a cheap plastic frame on the wall. A small wooden shoe, painted in red, white and blue, was perched on the napkin dispenser. A clean espresso cup sat on a saucer with two sugar cubes wrapped in paper next to a small plastic wrapped biscotti.

The barista (baristo? Danny would have to investigate) looked over to them as the wooden door squeaked closed.

"Stephen, Danny. What's up?" Eduardo started making their standard two double espressos in small ceramic cups.

"The Tut! Nothing much," Danny said and grinned at the slightly diminutive owner/barista. The Yobars had met The Tut the first week the coffee shop opened and he was a big reason that they were regulars. The Tut was sixtyish, about five foot four, and hailed from Spain (via Germany if his last

41

name was an indicator). He was thoroughly enjoying his new retirement occupation.

Stephen walked to the bar and responded, "Nothing much going on." A slight pause. "But is that, Tut, uncommon?" 'Uncommon' came out as 'Ankhamen'.

The Tut winced and then pointed to a quart sized tip jar on the counter and said, "I'm gonna put out a jar just for people who make King Tut jokes – what the hell, who make any puns - one dollar fine for each offense. You'll make me a rich fucking man."

"Dad, that's not even the first time you tried that one", Danny shook his head slightly and delivered the critique as if to one of his sophomore students. Danny had to remind himself that criticizing his dad's jokes was ineffective; in fact, it just encouraged him. When the Tut placed the two coffees in front of him, Danny sugared and creamed them and carried the two demitas cups on their demitas saucers over to their usual spot by the window. Stephen solemnly put a dollar in the tip jar.

Their window table had the best view in the shop. That is to say, it had the only view that didn't look out only on the parking lot. The Tut had planted a row of trees to block more of the parking lot, but they were young and didn't do much of a job yet.

Two Hispanic construction workers walked up to the bar and ordered two coffees. One carried a white paper package branded with the logo of the meat market next door. They sat down at the table behind Danny and Stephen and spoke in Spanish.

"What are you going to do with that kidney out in the heat for the rest of the day?" He pointed to his friend's white wrapped package, about the size of a fish. The friend smiled, "No problem. I have an ice cooler in the truck."

Stephen looked straight ahead, eavesdropping on the table behind him. *Sotto voce* to Danny: "What did they say? I only caught a few words." Danny hated it when people asked him to interpret a stranger's Spanish conversations. He rolled his eyes, but away from his dad. "Something about a cooking a kidney tonight. And ice. How the hell do I know?"

Stephen rallied. "How do you like that website management tool I showed you?"

"I have to say it's pretty great. I've been using it for about a week," Danny said. "I can identify any computer making contact with our network. Those charts are awesome."

Danny sipped his coffee. "I got the god password from Ted and we rebuilt the server and the email attacks seem to have stopped. We'll be ready next time."

They were quiet for a minute and then Stephen began to hear a soft, high pitched buzz. He tilted his head 45 degrees to the right and stared off blankly, trying to listen more intently.

"Can you hear that?" he said to Danny. Danny tilted his head obediently, listened intently, and said, "No, what is it?"

Stephen turned his head to the left and listened harder.

In between the sounds of nothing in the room, trillions of small looped dimensions vibrated with high energy packets which had been released during the Big Bang. In those first moments after the birth of the universe, the energy exploded through expanding space-time, free from all binds. At the end of the first moment in the life of the universe, many of those high energy packets absorbed into the small dimensional loops like water into a sponge. The energy packets whirled inside the dimensional loops like perfectly balanced Hot Wheels cars banking in a circular yellow plastic track. The few energy packets that escaped this fate had cooled down and presented Stephen with the universe.

"Nothing," Stephen said, shaking his head once. "I guess it is nothing."

After a moment, Stephen said, "Here's a joke for you." He paused. "Did you hear about the new erectile dysfunction pill? It's called mycocsafloppin."

Danny laughed. "OK. That one's good, you must not have made it up. Where did you hear it?"

"At the user's group meeting last month," Stephen said abashedly. "Who knew that pharma data managers had a sense of humor?"

"Not me," Danny replied. "I've never found that data managers had much of a sense of humor at all."

Stephen smiled at Danny. "Now, now, son, I can't get riled that easily. This *is* the treasurer of the RTP Clinical Data Managers User Group you're speaking to. Actually, it's the statisticians that don't have much of a sense of humor. By the time I've moved on to a new joke, they're still analyzing the first joke trying to determine if there is a 95% chance that it has not been proven to be non-funny. Cross-sectionally speaking, of course."

"Wow, these data manager support groups sound like a lot of fun." Danny sipped his espresso. Icy stare back from Stephen.

But Danny had been taught to rally by his dad. Change the subject.

"What are statisticians doing at a data management ..uh.. whatever?"

"Trying to steal our glory?" Stephen looked at the ceiling and slowly shook his head. "No, the users group is open to all," he continued magnanimously, lifting both arms and open palms upwards.

Stephen let his arms down. "It's mostly data managers from pharma companies in RTP, a few non-profit companies thrown in for good measure. The statisticians usually come when we have talks about standard formats for submitting data to the FDA. Lately, there's been a lot of clinical research associates, monitor types, attending because we've had demos on how to use web EDC data management systems."

Stephen leaned his head back mockingly and said, "Dare I ask about Barb again?"

"Brenda is doing fine. We've had a few more dates and we're getting along pretty well. Thanks for asking."

After an odd moment, Danny said, "Going back to work, Dad?"

"No, I'm treating myself to a matinee of the old computer movie 'Tron' at the dollar movie theater."

The Tut had drifted to Stephen and Danny's table, wiping down tables as he approached.

"Tut", Danny explained, "my dad is a geek from way back, back when that first Tron movie was released." Danny turned back to his father. "How come you're seeing the old movie, and not the new one? Did you hear something bad about the new 'Tron' movie, Dad?"

Stephen kept a straight face and said, "I haven't heard anything positive, or negative, about the new 'Tron'…. movie." Then his eyes got wide and he said, "Did you get that? 'Neutron'? Oooohhhh."

Danny hid his smile by finishing his coffee quickly, violating his father's rule that they pretend that they're sipping like Parisians at a café on Boulevard St. Germain. His eye wandered to the pastries under the glass cover by the cash register. "Do you think male baristas should be called baristos?"

"That's a damn good question." Stephen took out his smart phone and started googling 'baristo'. Danny stood and walked back to the bar. This 'baristo' issue had the triple effect of stopping the data management conversation, creating a diversion so that he could get a pastry without admonishment, and actually settling the baristo/a quandary. Which he could use on a school quiz – that makes it quadruple! A sure sign that it was better to buy two pastries rather than to split one.

Chapter 7 – March 21

The Deli Pail was one of the few RTP eateries that had charm, albeit a tacky charm. Patrons parked in a gravel lot and entered through a covered porch into the cinder block building. The restaurant held several tables and benches, a beverage container with decent beer, and a line which moved slowly towards the order counter. After placing their order, the experienced customers headed to the real charm of The Deli Pail: the seating in the back yard. Out of view of the busy road, approximately two acres of cut grass hosted wooden picnic tables encircled by tall Carolina pines. A small pond in the shade gave way to paths of soft dirt which led through the woods.

Alexandria was sitting at an off kilter picnic table, enjoying the sunshine of the early afternoon. It was almost the end of March, but it was a warm day in the upper 60s. She had shed her CEO image, converting to sandals, comfortable jeans, and a loosely fitting shirt buttoned to the top. After a few minutes of listening to the PA system announcing orders to be picked up at the counter, Alexandria saw Blake Roth walk into the back area and slowly scan the yard for her. As she'd guessed, he was wearing his suit and tie for their post-lunch trip to the NC Museum of Art. Blue looked good on him, she thought, even if he couldn't do casual.

She enjoyed watching him look for her. When he smiled at her in recognition, she felt a flash of energy and happiness. This wasn't wrong, she thought, it was right. She stood up and walked towards him. When they met, their hug lingered longer than at the conclusion of their last date. His lips grazed her cheek, and she released the hug with a quick squeeze. They went inside, ordered, and came back to their bench.

Though they had seen each other several times over the past few weeks, she was still a little nervous that someone would see them holding hands. People from his company, her company, her old network of friends: you never knew who was watching in the small community of RTP.

She smiled at him and flipped his tie up. "You always seem so ..... serious," Alexandria started. "Don't you ever have any fun?"

"Well, I was quite the cut-up in med school," Blake parried.

"Such as?"

Blake raised his eyes to the sky and pretended to think hard to cover his sadness that his 'cut-up' joke hadn't worked. "Well, there was this one time. Someone was stealing food out of the refrigerator in our lab and we couldn't figure out who. So one day before we left the lab, we put some phenolphthalein, a laxative, into a sandwich in the fridge. The next morning, the sandwich was gone but there were tell-tale signs that the laxative had worked. Rapidly."

Alexandria laughed. "How did you get that phenyl, whatever it was?"

He enjoyed making her laugh; he didn't have that effect on everyone.

"Oh, it's a common reagent that's available in most labs. It's a buffer for determining the pH of..." Her laugh faded off and he realized he was boring her now. "I had you, then I lost you," Blake said ruefully. "Such is the fate of a researcher, I suppose."

She laughed again. "That's OK. I owe you for listening to my lab data transfer stories."

He leaned forward and said, "You seem pretty serious yourself. What do you do for fun?" He slouched back on the backless picnic bench and then tried to straighten up to closely follow her answer.

The look on her face showed that a deep answer was not forthcoming.

She brightly answered, "Let's see, what am I up to these days? My passwords, for one. This week it is a haiku, last week it was an acrostic of the first letters each line in Shakespeare's 18th sonnet. Who knows next week? That's my fun."

He smiled and gave her a quick kiss over the picnic table.

It was 1:30PM by the time their food was ready, and when they had finished eating forty five minutes later, there were only a few other people lingering in the back area. When they had disposed of their eating utensils, Blake suggested they walk to the pond.

The new moon was pale and full in the sky. There were no clouds and the weather was perfect. They circled around the pond on a soft path that led into the woods. She thought he seemed genuinely interested as they talked about the green and purple flowers floating on the still water. He pointed to the dragonflies in the pond's shadowy back corner.

When she thought back on it over the next few days, she truly couldn't remember how they gravitated to one of the back paths. But within a few minutes, they were deep in the woods, sitting on a fallen tree, in the silence of buzzing insects. Their hands moved gently from holding to hugging, channeling their emotions through their fingers. More wonderfully, she didn't feel like she had to speak as she had spoken so many times with previous lovers. When they kissed, his lips tasted of blackberry soda and he had a clean scent about him. When she placed her hand behind his neck and pulled him closer for a longer kiss, he responded gently. When she slowed down, he slowed down with her and they floated.

The seclusion of the woods, the search and discovery of their natural beauty, and the exhilaration of a clear conscience led to events that soon left them catching their breath. Sitting and hugging again on the fallen tree, their hands once again expressed what they couldn't yet say. She leaned against him and held her head still. The edge of the moon appeared to touch one of the tree branches. She took five slow breaths and felt that she could actually see the moon move in a groove in the sky, like a ball spinning in a roulette wheel. She took a deep breath, let out one last sigh, and stood up on knees that were now pretty wobbly. They hugged, straightened their clothes, and slowly walked back to the pond. They made a pit stop in the restaurant bathrooms before going to their cars. She would follow his car to the museum, they decided. As she started her car, she decided that her first sexual encounter with a man in twelve years turned out better than she dared imagine.

"A 'cut up in med school'," she repeated out loud in her car. She shook her head and looked at herself in the mirror.

"Jesus, what have I gotten myself into?"

Chapter 8 – April 15

Renae Daye could always tell when her boss was arriving. The high rev of the engine, the short squeal of the tires, and finally the slam of the metal door heralded the arrival of the executive to whom she was the assistant. As executive assistant, she knew that Dr. Moore liked to get off to a quick start to the day. Today, a telephone conference at 9AM that was just a half an hour away from starting.

Renae unconsciously patted down the thick curls of brown hair that protruded from her head. She had the daily folder ready to hand him as he entered the office.

"Good morning", Arthur Moore said as he took off and hung up his rain coat.

"Good morning, Dr. Moore", Renae replied. "Here is today's schedule. I'm going to start the conference call in a few minutes and I'll put the phone on mute. There is a fresh pot of coffee and a few things from the bakery." She pointed to the coffee station near her desk.

Arthur said thank you and took coffee and a chocolate filled croissant. Before going to his office, he looked at the vase of flowers on Renae's desk and said, "Those flowers look nice. Your husband is very thoughtful."

She smiled and looked at the vase. The flowers were nice, but they were 'get out of the doghouse' flowers. Her forty third birthday had passed without any presents, unless you counted the pair of running socks he gave her, which apparently he *did* count but she did not. But it had been a busy time for her husband, what with getting the new sixty four inch plasma TV mounted in time for baseball season, and all.

She kept smiling. "Yes, he is very thoughtful."

Arthur smiled once more and walked to his office. His office spanned half the side of the building. There were several large windows on the southern exposure but the conference table was further down next to a wall covered with his diplomas and awards.

He sat at his desk and opened his email looking for any last minute documents for the meeting. He saw an email with an attachment from Erik Lindisfarne from the venture capitalist firm Holly and McLoud. The file was named "AMP third wave investment.xlsx" and Arthur quickly opened it. The new terms from H&M were for less capital than he needed at a steeper price than he wanted. H&M was losing patience. But Arthur was more upset that the formulas and values shown on the spreadsheet were unformatted. Didn't even have dollar signs or commas. This is the kind of crap they show a CEO of a rising pharma biotech?

He printed the spreadsheets and moved to the conference table where the conference call was on hold and muted. After a few moments, Arthur could hear muffled movement and chatter on the other end of the line. At 9AM sharp, he unmuted and spoke clearly into the phone.

"Good morning, Erik. This is Arthur. How are you this morning?"

"We're doing well here, Arthur. We hope you are too. I've got a few people from finance here with me this morning. You remember Ken from the first round of funding. Did you get my email with the new numbers for wave three of funding?"

"Yes," Arthur said looking again at the unattractively formatted printouts. "I couldn't help but notice that things have changed since we last talked."

After a pause, Lindisfarne said, "Arthur, H&M has $12 million invested in AMP; we're the largest investor. We're five years in and we're still looking for that home run. Now, the malaria vaccines are progressing nicely, and we have high hopes for this HIV safety trial you're running, real high hopes. That's why we're funding wave three. But we can't put in as much and we can't have as high a risk this time."

Arthur spoke confidently to the phone. "The HIV safety study is already started – our main site in Philadelphia is open. We have a few weeks of data in and there are no problems. I have to start planning *now* for a Phase III multicenter study that will prove efficacy. That's going take about..." He stared at the ceiling and calculated. "... about five million more than this wave three offer."

Lindisfarne either didn't say anything or he was on mute on the other end discussing.

Arthur pressed on with his sales pitch. "H&M is going to quadruple its investment when this drug pays off. I know it will. The malaria resistance genetics I saw in Tanzania fifteen years ago showed me how to fight off the HIV virus. It worked in the animal safety studies. It's working now in the safety study. I know it will work. When the results from the multinational efficacy trial are published, AMP is going to be worth 100 million."

Another moment of silence passed. Lindisfarne returned to the line.

"Okay Arthur. We'll put the five million back in. Luis will send you the revised file this afternoon. But I want a copy of the monthly progress report for the trial. I want them on the tenth of every month until you publish the clinical study report."

They said goodbye and Arthur disconnected the call.

He went back to his desk and logged onto the trial's EDC system. He was going to look at every report and every table just to make sure nothing was going wrong.

Chapter 9 - May 1

By the beginning of May, the cold in Philadelphia had just begun to fade. Alexandria Knott arrived on a 7:50AM flight out of RDU. She stood outside the terminal and waited briefly for a rental car van to take her to her car. After loading bags into the back of the van, she and five others huddled inside on benches, three to a side, tête-à-tête, in the cramped quarters. There was a local AM radio station playing over the speakers, but mostly in the front by the driver. The man sitting a foot across from Alexandria took out his cell phone and began talking to his friend, who knows where.

"Nothing much, what are you doing?....No, I'm in the rental car van.... The new job is doing well. I don't have to do much yet, so it's pretty sweet...I get a laptop *and* a phone, dude....." Thank God it was only a few minutes to the car, she thought.

Alexandria walked directly to her car, got inside, and oriented herself. She brought her own GPS because it gave her traffic updates and re-routed her when necessary. She set the GPS for the clinic, though she'd been there once already for the study.

Twenty minutes of driving through Philadelphia was enough to satisfy Alexandria's desire to view the cityscape. An hour later she was looking at green hills and white fences, at least some of the time. By 2PM she was pulling into the visitors section of the clinic parking lot. She put her phone and GPS in her purse and rolled her small luggage bag into the lobby. The security guard viewed Alexandria's ID and gave her a visitor's badge. The guard then took her bag, purse, and laptop and placed them in a locked room behind the guard station. Alexandria thanked her and walked up to the second floor.

Alexandria was met at the top of the stairs by the site investigator and study coordinator. The site investigator, Dr. Earl Godwin, ran the clinic and usually two or three (lucrative) clinical trials at a time. Alexandria judged him to be in his mid fifties, based on his graying hair, slight paunch, and of course his *curriculum vitae* which she reviewed when she started the study. He had hazel eyes and a very reassuring smile that Alexandria bought totally, even though she knew it must have been his bedside manner smile. The study coordinator, a registered nurse named Natalie Everett, ran all the trials at the clinic, including this one. Natalie Everett was late thirties and had a tremendous amount of energy, too much for Alexandria's personal taste, but very effective for a study coordinator. Natalie had brownish hair worn in a Farrah Fawcette-esque cut, though she probably was unfamiliar with Farrah. She had the faint scent of cigarette smoke. Her dark black eyes were active and her smile very friendly; she was a compulsive smiler. Alexandria played the mental game 'Do they or don't they' with Godwin and Natalie but couldn't come up with a clear answer.

Dr. Godwin is what is known as a 'paper' site investigator because he functioned mostly by signing his name on papers. Nurse Everett kept track of trial documents, data collected during the trial, answered queries about the data, and managed recruitment for the trial. What she didn't do, Alexandria did. Godwin was a successful investigator because he has a good supply of potential clinical trial participants and he published one or two papers a year. The clinic was located near several retirement communities and universities which provided trials like this with a supply of healthy volunteers (in search of money) to determine the pharmacokinetics and pharmacodynamics of the AMP vaccine.

After hellos, Dr. Godwin asked with formality, "Alexandria, do you have a telephone, laptop computer or any computer with you in the clinic area during this visit?" Dr. Godwin's subagreement with AMP required him to ask this of all visitors to the clinic related to this trial. Arthur Moore's instructions on this point were explicit: this trial was to have no paper used and no other electronic versions besides the official study database being hosted at headquarters in RTP.

Just as formally, Alexandria responded, "No, I do not." And she didn't; they were with the security guard downstairs.

Dr. Godwin, Nurse Everett, and Alexandria gathered around a round wooden table in Godwin's office. Several glasses and a large goblet of water were in the middle of the table. They had a late afternoon coffee, mostly out of deference to Alexandria who had been traveling all day and faced four hours in the office before heading to the hotel tonight. A full day's work awaited her the next day.

Their standard meeting agenda included the status of the trial, the recruitment rates, regulatory requirements, and any new problems that might soon become serious adverse events. The study was going smoothly with no problems, and more importantly, no SAEs. After the hour long briefing, they stood and went their separate ways for the evening, agreeing to meet again at the table at 8AM tomorrow.

First, Alexandria monitored the regulatory files in the study coordinator's office. She compared the contents of the files to the requirements in the International Conference on Harmonization's E6 Good Clinical Practices. All the files were in perfect order and up to date – mostly because Alexandria herself set up the file structure and made sure that it was in compliance even when she was not on site. She logged into the study trial management system and entered her results into the 'monitoring visit' module that existed alongside and interlaced with the clinical database EDC system.

After the regulatory file check, Alexandria's next task was to monitor the participant's files. This is where the site kept original notes and observations regarding each participant. No personal identifiers were contained in this file; all of its contents were labeled only with a five digit participant identification code. After being captured in the medical charts, participant data was usually formatted onto paper case report forms for entry into the clinical trial database system. She instinctively looked for the file cabinets containing paper source documents and case report forms before being reminded again that no such paper charts existed: all the information was stored in 'electronic' case report forms in the EDC clinical database hosted at AMP's facility in RTP.

When she logged into the EDC system, the database categorized and recorded her actions: the time she logged in, the reports she ran, the menu options she selected, the subject data pages she viewed. Everything. She had to admit that the best part of the system was that it created a trip report while she was working; that saved many hours back at the office. She could add commentary and edit the report, including the action items for the site staff.

Finished with site management information, Alexandria logged into the clinical data side of the EDC system. Her password was accepted but the system prompted her to change it immediately because the password hadn't been changed in four weeks. That kind of security was fine with her because she had no trouble remembering passwords, not for any of the twenty or so accounts she had, from WDM accounts to project accounts like this to her personal financial web sites. She thought of it as her savant talent. Not the best talent, but a very useful one for saving time in the computer world. She smiled as she entered her new password.

Alexandria ran the standard reports from the software dashboard and sent them to the trip report. These reports compared the actual rates of enrollment to the goals in the recruitment plan for the site. As was common, this clinic was not recruiting at the planned rate, but the numbers were headed in the right direction. The clinic was paid for each participant enrolled, each participant visit, each sample sent to the lab. The site PI was given a bonus for each participant closed with a 'Final completion' status, meaning that all their expected data was present and that there were no unresolved queries.

Queries were the bane of all clinical trial data management systems. When data is entered into the EDC system, it is compared to a set of acceptable values and logically compared to other data in the system for that participant. If the data is discrepant with these data cleaning rules, then the system alerts the person entering the data. This is called a query. The person entering the data can change the data to a more acceptable value or leave the value as it was and enter a reason why the data is correct even if the EDC system thinks that it is incorrect. Any change in the data is automatically tracked in a permanent audit trail. All information regarding the query is audited also, including a record of who viewed the query, comments back and forth between the site staff and the monitor, and the final resolution status of the query. Depending upon the biostatisticians and data programmers specifying the data cleaning rules, a trial can generate thousands of queries that take site staff and monitors weeks to manage.

Alexandria went into the EDC system 'Monitor participant' mode and was greeted with a very colorful screen. Each participant had one row of status indicators going across the screen from left to right. Each column represented a study visit, like 'Screening Visit', 'Enrollment Visit', and 'Final Visit'. There was also a column to indicate the presence of unscheduled visits. The last column indicated the presence of forms not related to a specific visit, such as an adverse event form or a medication form.

A bright green check mark appeared if a participant had no data problems outstanding with their data for that particular visit. An orange question mark appeared if there were open queries. If the data was not expected yet, a faded out gray circle would appear. Happily, there were no red exclamation points indicating overdue queries or serious adverse events.

An adverse event, defined by the same ICH GCP that Alexandria used to check the regulatory files, is any new or worsening untoward medical event that occurs to the participant. Each adverse event is judged by the study medical monitor to determine if the event were related to the clinical trial, to determine the highest severity of the event (mild, moderate, severe), and most importantly, its seriousness. If the adverse event were serious, it is then classified as a Serious Adverse Event (Alexandria gave the ICH no points for cleverness on that nomenclature). An SAE was bad news for a participant, and even worse news for the clinical trial. As soon as an SAE is detected, the site investigator is obliged by federal law to inform the safety authorities for the trial. SAE's which can be identified before data is entered into the EDC system must be reported manually by the site investigators.

Her next task was to look for new adverse events. There were a few lab values slightly out of range but not abnormal enough to trigger the system to generate an automatic query. She wanted to follow them closely.

Alexandria looked behind her to see if anyone was watching; no one was there. She reached into her pocket and took out her lipstick case. One more look, still no one. Instead of taking off the top and applying the bright red lipstick, she exposed the camera lens, pointed it at the screen, and pushed the picture button with her right index finger. This camera/USB drive/lipstick case was a give-away at the Drug Information Association meeting two years ago in San Diego. It would hold about fifty pictures. She took pictures of all the screens with lab data nearly out of range. She looked over her shoulder again and put away the lipstick case.

Yes, she trusted the EDC system, but only up to a point. It couldn't hurt to have a backup. If this 'totally electronic' trial didn't work, then it would look bad for her company too just by association. She wasn't going to put her company at risk just because of some overzealous pharma exec.

Chapter 10 – May 25 - Danny

At 8PM on Friday, I met Bob and Christina at 'Chicken and Waffles' in downtown Durham on Main St. The plan was to eat and then go dancing. Brenda was out of town for the Memorial Day weekend so it was just the three of us.

It wasn't long after we were seated that Bob started in on Brenda and me.

He puffed up his chest and announced, "When you've been engaged as long as I have, you become an expert in these matters. Right, Christina?"

Christina laughed and said, "Sure Bob. Anything you say. But your engagement is going to be less than a year - 'cause it's about to end in a few months!"

Bob turned back to me and said, "So what's the Brenda situation?"

"Pretty good," I responded. "We're doing pretty well."

"I can't help but notice that she's not here this weekend, so you're not doing well enough to spend holidays together yet," he replied.

"I was going to go to Minnesota with her but it just didn't work out." It didn't work out because I was too nervous to meet her parents. Too soon. But the truth was that I was a little scared.

Christina could read between the lines. "First you were going to go with her, then you told her we had some phantom gig, then you said you could maybe go. Sounds to me like she got tired of seeing you flip flop and she made an executive decision."

Bob scrunched his eyebrows in a way that was supposed to make me think he was being serious.

"We don't want to see a replay of your last relationship."

I replied quickly (too quickly?), "That was totally different. We were only dating for two months and she was almost ready to move in." Actually, it was too bad about that; I really did like her. I could feel my face giving too much away so I ended with, "Yeah, she overplayed her hand and that was that."

"That may be, but the reality was that it left you overplaying your hand, if memory serves," Bob zinged me. Christina laughed.

"Great", I said. "Now your jokes are almost as good as my dad's."

After eating, we walked across the street and passed by the ten feet tall bronze bull statue. The charging bull represented Durham, The Bull City. It was a local landmark.

I stopped and patted the bull.

"Guys", I furrowed my brow and said to them with concern, "in case we get separated tonight, we can meet up here, OK?" Their only response was to walk a little faster.

We got to the dance bar around 9:30PM, perhaps a little too early. We kind of hung to the side for a while.

Christina made the first move. "Come on! I came here to dance, not stand around!" She pulled Bob out with her into the music, and I instinctively joined them in the small crowd. Though I tried to dance along with them, I was inevitably separated and soon I was dancing alone. I didn't know if it were me being a little self conscious, or maybe this place was a little uptight, but the fun quotient wasn't rising.

These kids came up to Christina. Apparently they knew each other from UNC and it turns out the 'kids' were in their early 20s. As I came over, the young woman in the group said, "This place is no good for dancing. We're going to another club. Do you want to come with us?"

As I was giving my slow nod, 'Hey, I'm thinking about that' face I used to hide the fact that I had already decided 'no', they were all headed out the door. So I followed.

We walked about fifteen minutes and it was really a rather pleasant walk. We transitioned from the downtown restaurant zone to the industrial zone by going down Rigsbee St. The air was slightly cool and the sky was clear. Downtown Durham did have some interesting architecture and this wasn't a vantage point I'd seen it from often.

The warehouse district was lined with fences topped with razor wire to prevent people from personally depositing litter in the vacant lots rather than having the wind do their job. A few micro pubs appeared and soon people were flowing onto the streets, eating nouveau cuisine from food trucks.

We approached Motorco, a cool bar with a great stage that featured local music almost every night. At first glance, Motorco had two bar areas that were open to the sidewalk. At second glance, I could see the garage doors that would pull down and lock at closing time. Classic rock karaoke was being perpetrated in the converted garages. Some of the kids at the Durham Friends School played on the main stage inside last summer.

But we didn't go into Motorco. We passed it and walked towards a medium sized ranch house next to a vacant lot across the street. It looked like an old house that hadn't gotten the memo that the neighborhood had died. As we got closer I could see that it was put together better than it looked. Someone had painted the walls of the house to match the shingles – very monochromatic. Slowly strobing colored light glowed from the front windows. The blaring music let me know it was a club. That, and the sign on the lawn that said 'Leslie's Lounge'.

The kids opened the door into the music and sauntered straight onto the jammed dance floor. We elders had to get our hand stamped. I put in three fives for the cover for all three of us. One for all and all for one.

The music was thumping and the crowd was raucous. We went into the mob, and I noticed something. Almost all the dancers were female.

I felt the fun quotient start to go up.

The atmosphere just radiated 'Friday night'. The lighting wasn't over the top and the music vibe was relaxed energy. I was dancing like a madman. I found a groove and I was sticking with it. All around me were women gyrating, shaking their hips, flowing their arms and hands.

Upon further review, the fun quotient dropped as I realized that I was dancing in a lesbian bar.

When the music stopped for a moment, Bob turned to me and said, "How do you like this place, man?"

I said, "It's awesome. This bar is more fun than that first dive. Let's see if I can get a Mojito done my way."

I side stepped my way through the crowd to the bar, a not altogether unpleasant experience. I ordered a mojito, a beer for Bob, and a glass of white wine for Christina. They got to the bar a few moments later. We clinked our glasses, and said, "Cheers!"

The music turned to rock and roll. A rockabilly tune came on from 'Crazy Kavan & The Rhythm Rockers'. I'd only heard of them recently from a story PBS radio did on them a few months back.

I took a sip from my mojito. I had ordered top shelf rum, and it was way, way bold.

Chapter 11 – August 30

Thad Jones drove Taxi #24 down the two lane country road, slowed, and turned left into the grape orchard. A gravel driveway wound towards an entrance into the parking lot/pasture. After parking along the white fence, he armed himself with a five gallon bucket and picked muscadine grapes for fifteen minutes straight. He only paused loading his bucket to eat grape after succulent grape. Thad paid and left the change from his $20 when he eyed the long, white watchdog hunkered down at the checkout table.

Five minutes and ten grapes later, Jones was back to work, taking I-40 towards RDU airport. Fifteen minutes and twenty more grapes later, he pulled into the pickup zone at Terminal A. Arthur Moore got in and put his small rolling carry-on bag onto the rear seat behind the driver. "Durham Bulls Athletic Park, please," he said from the rear of the taxi. His voice was smooth and authoritative. Jones would have been impressed except that he couldn't really think about anything besides that bag of disappearing grapes on the front passenger's seat. With the windows rolled up, the cab smelled like the grape orchard.

Taxi #24 took I-40 west to the Durham Freeway north and exited at the sign 'Durham Bulls Athletic Park'. The DBAP was the new stadium for the Durham Bulls, not the old stadium in the movie 'Bull Durham'. It was impressive, perhaps a little too impressive, as the cost was voted down by the taxpayers of Durham. Luckily for the voters in Durham, the City Council knew better and decided that the stadium should be funded anyway. Maybe they were right; downtown Durham was flourishing in spots, especially around the DBAP complex.

After picking up his ticket at Will Call, Arthur turnstiled his way into the park and asked an usher for directions to the picnic area. The usher pointed down the third base line and said follow the signs up the stairs to the corporate picnic area. First though, Arthur bought a Durham Bulls cap to keep the sun off his pate.

Before heading to the picnic area, Arthur detoured up to the field level behind home plate. He walked slowly up the steep ramp and looked into the open stadium. The sky, outfield grass, infield dirt, and baselines spectrumed through deep blues, bright greens, soft browns, and brilliant whites.

Arthur returned to the cement tarmac and walked to the picnic area. The sign said 'AMP Summer Company Picnic'. The rollers on his suitcase echoed loudly as he pulled it through the short, narrow tunnel leading to the picnic area. It was the bottom of the third inning and the party was well underway. He weaved his way through the crowd with a big smile and his new Durham Bulls cap. Looking for a place to put his bag, he said hello's and how are you's to his employees. Renae Daye was with her husband sitting on a bench eating. Arthur settled on the rear corner where the caterers had placed several of their transportation containers. He passed on the catered food initially and decided instead to go in search of a hot dog necessary to complete his baseball park visit.

Walking out the narrow tunnel, Arthur said hello to Tammy Rose as she entered the tunnel pushing her brightly colored ice cream cart towards the entrance of the picnic area. The cart vaguely reminded Arthur of a scene in a Marx Brothers movie.

The side of the aluminum cart was emblazoned with the store's name 'Renata's on Ninth Street' in diagonal red script reminiscent of the style used by the Atlanta Braves.

Tammy easily propelled the large wheeled cart by pushing on a horizontal bar on the back. The push bar was adorned with bells and miniature wind chimes to satisfy the customers' desire to associate bells with ice cream.

Tammy's ice cream was the official dessert of the picnic. She placed a white sign on the cart proclaiming that she was serving Renata's best sellers: Mexican chocolate, French vanilla, coffee with chips, and lemon ice cream. Alexandria walked nonchalantly to the ice cream stand before the crowd noticed that Tammy was there.

Tammy straightened her apron, and looked up at Alexandria. "Can I get you something you'd like?" Tammy smiled as sexily as she could in public.

Alexandria looked over her shoulder nervously, then said, "I'd like for you to cool off." Then, with a smile, "And my favorite, almond ice cream in a cup." She looked again to make sure they were alone.

Tammy reached to the back of the freezer and extracted a pint container with the letter 'A' written on the lid. "I always bring a special container of your favorite – almond for Allie." She served a cup and handed it to Alexandria with a wooden spoon and paper napkin. Her fingertips lingered on Alexandria's hand during the delivery. Now, just like she had planned, with her stomach tightening as she looked for her voice, Tammy said to her former lover. "I miss you. Can we get together for dinner? It will be fun, I promise."

Alexandria flinched a little at the words but answered sympathetically. "Tammy. It's been a year now. Come on, it's over. All we ever did was get together, break up, get together. I'm sorry, but I've moved on for good now. Please, let's talk about something else." She nervously put the spoon in the ice cream and ate. She looked over her right shoulder and they were still alone.

"How is Janice? I haven't been to the book store for a long time." Alexandria asked, hoping to turn the conversation from the past to the present.

Tammy didn't like the new topic. She closed the top door of the freezer abruptly. "Janice? She's fine."

For all of about five seconds, Tammy held it in, her face turning redder and redder and her stomach sinking lower and lower. She asked it over and over in her mind until she could resist asking. "How is that Blake? Why don't you introduce us all to your beloved new Blake?" Tammy was shocked at the strident tone of her own voice ringing in the tunnel.

Alexandria stepped back slightly and responded in a harsh tone. "He's not here, which is the only reason I came knowing you would be here. I recommended you for this party because I thought we could just talk and start to be friends again. What is your problem?"

Alexandria's voice started to crack but she pushed on. "God, what was I thinking? We are so over. You were understanding enough when I was with you. You encouraged me to be who I was, not just who others thought I was supposed to be."

Alexandria stopped for a moment but felt she had to continue. "Now that I'm something you *don't* approve of, you are very not-understanding, very judgmental, and very mean." She started to cry and threw her cup of almond ice cream into a garbage can. Alexandria stalked back into the crowded picnic.

Tammy bent down behind the cart and pretended to rearrange stock while she wiped her eyes.

The hot dog condiment station was just around the corner on the tarmac within listening distance of the ice cream stand. They were more intruding on him than he was eavesdropping on them, he thought. Arthur Moore turned the corner into the narrow tunnel. He passed the ice cream cart holding two freshly mustarded hot dogs and sporting a bemused smirk on his face.

Chapter 12 – September 6

Alexandria was nervous as she drove to meet Blake for dinner. The data irregularities she had seen in the EDC system on her most recent monitoring visit had thrown a wrench into the works of their new relationship. She hadn't figured out how to tell him. Maybe the irregularities weren't even a problem. But maybe they were. But maybe she was wrong. She shook her head. This dinner could be their first big argument and she didn't know which way he would go when push came to shove.

Alexandria had invited Blake to dinner at the Parizade restaurant in Durham. A good choice because they had eaten there several times and they always had a great time. Parizade was in the ground floor of Erwin Square, an upscale strip mall punctuated by a four story building with the foundation of a twenty story building. Blake told her it looked like they lost their building permit once they got four stories up. She smiled to herself – Blake did have a way of making her laugh.

Blake, she thought, as she parked around the corner from Parizade. She took the keys out of the ignition and sat inside the car, listening to the ticking of the engine. These butterflies in my stomach are beginning to wear thin, she thought as she finally exited. She walked briskly to the restaurant, barely noticing her wavy doppelganger shadowing her in the store windows she passed. Her purse was clutched tightly as she entered the lobby and saw Blake waiting for her.

Blake was dressed in his work uniform of suit and tie. His thin wavy brown hair was hardly mussed but the beginnings of a 5 o'clock shadow appeared on his jaw. He smiled at her and she felt welcome. They met with a hug and a kiss.

They walked through the lobby and Blake asked the maître d' if they could get a table outside. Alexandria nodded her agreement to the maître d'.

An elegant looking man in a dark suit and black tie approached the podium. Ivan was of European descent, possibly near the Adriatic. He was thirty two with short black hair not worn in an American style. He reminded Alexandria of a dancer: slender, athletic, always moving his arms or shifting his weight. His face was constantly smiling to one degree or another. A beautiful accent wove through his words and gestures. He was a true professional and he treated himself and his patrons with respect.

Ivan had been their waiter on their previous dates and he welcomed them graciously.

"Welcome to Parizade, my friends. It is good to see you again." Ivan shook hands with Blake and gave Alexandria a small kiss on both cheeks.

"Ivan, are there any tables outside tonight? Is that live music in the courtyard?", Blake asked.

"Of course, of course. Let me take you," Ivan replied and led them to a courtyard behind the restaurant. The late summer night was unseasonably warm and the moon was three quarters full and nearly directly overhead. Ivan bounced quickly to a table with a good view of the band. Half of the courtyard's ten tables were occupied.

Ivan pulled out a chair for Alexandria. Alexandria looked over to the jazz trio. A grizzled old saxophone player was singing out notes with beautiful tones that echoed off the courtyard walls. The drummer was just a young man, looking to the side with half closed eyes while laid down the beat. The bass player was younger and female which surprised her.

A server placed water, bread, and a small tray with olive oil and spices on the table and took their order. Blake mixed the olive oil and spices together in a small dish while Alexandria ordered.

After some small talk, she turned the conversation to the trial and to the upcoming Data and Safety Monitoring Board meeting. The DSMB would look at the trial's data up through last month. Although the EDC system may be able to make data sets quickly with up to date data, it still takes four weeks to get the data to the DSMB. The statisticians needed two weeks to run the data into their table shells that they had previously created. Sometimes there were problems with the statistical table shells, sometimes with the data. The table shells deliberately looked at data from different angles, so it was possible that the reports would not be internally consistent if there were outstanding data queries that affected the tables. The DSMB members themselves wanted two weeks to review the statistical report. DSMB reports could highlight problems with efficacy or safety that would make the venture capitalist partners at AMP worried about the future of this vaccine.

She looked at Blake tentatively. "I'm worried about the DSMB report. I'm not sure the database reports are coming out of the clinical EDC system right and it could make us look bad." That was the best she could do to broach the topic of data changing.

Blake looked startled. "Why do you say that?" He was confident in the EDC system but he was becoming more and more confident of Alexandria as well.

She paused and tried not to blurt. "There could be a problem with the EDC database reports. Some data values seem like they are changing, but I can't confirm it when go back on my next site visit. Two monitoring visits ago, I saw some CD4 lab data at the low end of the normal range and I thought it would fire off a query, and generate a Serious Adverse Event, but that hasn't happened. When I went back last week, the data was all in the normal range and for all I could see in the EDC system, there never was any low values, even in the audit trail. I guess I could be mistaken though."

He tried, "Maybe you're getting the participants confused. There aren't any paper charts and it must be hard to keep track of individual lab results just from memory."

'Just from memory' – he's asking me if I've made any paper notes which is against her contract, she realized. Well, he's right - she had photos she'd taken with her lipstick camera. She even had a few on her phone now in case she wanted to show him.

She decided that the conversation had gone about as well as she could have hoped for and she chickened out of showing him the pictures.

"Lab data is my specialty, you will remember, but you're right," she said while trying to smile. "I'm just nervous about the study. I've hitched my company's wagon to this trial and I'm just a little nervous that the DSMB will find something wrong. Half my company is working on this trial." She reached for his hand and turned her head to the band.

Blake was reassuring. "Just bring it up at the next quarterly meeting with Dr. Moore and you'll see, I'm sure there is no problem. You're just worried."

She tried to give a reassuming look back, and said "You're probably right."

She caressed his hand, and turned to look at the band.

The band was playing soft music. The sky was clear but warm. A few minutes into the song, she realized that something was 'on' inside her. She felt happy and loved - this part was going well, at least. She squeezed Blake's hand but kept her eyes on the band. Nonverbal communication seemed to be the best thing for their relationship.

"You're probably right," she said again. She wasn't going to convince him. And maybe he was right, she thought, what am I, an EDC expert?

But she couldn't let it go. "Maybe I shouldn't do any more AMP studies. These 'all electronic, no paper' studies are too risky for me; I don't have all *that* much experience. Maybe I'm just not the right person for these EDC studies the way Dr. Moore wants to run them."

Blake was shocked and said, "But that will mean giving up this big chance for your company."

She looked him straight in the eye and after a few beats said, "There'll be more big chances, right? And you're not going away with the trials, are you?" Her adrenaline was pumping as she watched for his reaction which was a kiss.

LETTER TO THE EDITOR

"In regard to my girlfriend's recent comments ("You're not going away with the trials, are you?" and " problem with the EDC database reports"), how does she expect me to handle this double-barreled bombshell? What she described as happening in the database - the reports and the audit trail not working - couldn't have happened. But if she thinks I don't believe her about the database, then she will probably be angry with me. There's nothing in it for me to doubt the proper functioning of the EDC system. More importantly, it sounds like she's starting to feel the same things for me that I feel for her. But whenever I try to bring up the 'L' word, it seems like she starts to retreat. Maybe it will be better for her to say it to me first."   - Blake Roth, Durham

Chapter 13 – November 24

Around 6PM on the Saturday after Thanksgiving, Danny drove from Durham Friends School to his mother's house for her annual party. He kept the top down and it was cold but this would be one of the last days of the year for convertablization. The Spider navigated the back roads linking Durham County to downtown Chapel Hill. As dusk fell, Danny slowed through beautiful old Chapel Hill neighborhoods as he made his way to Franklin Street. He cruised past a cemetery with headstones dating back to the 1700's. You've really got to be somebody to get in there now, Danny thought. At the light, he turned away from the campus area and headed north on Franklin Street. There was no parking on this busy street, so even though his mother's house was a few blocks ahead on the right, he had to seek refuge in the city parking lot a block or so off Franklin Street. It was probably the prettiest city parking lot Danny had ever seen. A grove of beautiful old oaks and maples made way for gravel parking spaces anchored by landscape timbers which retained valuable soil. The trees didn't seem to begrudge the parking lot so Danny decided not to either.

His bottles of wine safely ensconced in a cotton grocery bag (Mom was on a 'green' kick lately), Danny walked back to Franklin Street and turned right. Soon, a driveway poked out to the main road, announcing itself with a wooden sign high on the driveway fence 'Tree Hill'. Up the driveway was a gazebo on the left and several cars parked on the right. Danny always enjoyed looking at the gazebo because it was his playhouse growing up. When he was three, his parents gave him the gazebo for Christmas and he remembered that it took them hours to assemble it. His mother had moved the gazebo when she migrated to Chapel Hill after the divorce. It jarred him now like a familiar memory in an unfamiliar setting.

His mother's house was gorgeous inside and out. The facade was large gray field stones. The roof was covered with solar panels facing the southern exposure. A huge oak door with a large window provided entrance to the house. He stepped into the foyer, took off his coat, and surveyed the party which was in full swing. The stairs were ahead to the right. Most of the action was in the kitchen and to the left in the living rooms. The food and drink tables were in the back next to the covered porch. Several coolers loaded with ice and beer lined the edge of the porch. A wooden door on a tight spring that snapped the door shut after every passage was the only way out of the porch to the woods. A small group of smokers lurked outside the porch under the green boughs of the woods leading down to the creek.

He passed through the door on the right into the TV room which he knew would be filled with kids watching videos or doing something else more entertaining than attending their parents' party. This was the only route which led to his favorite space in the whole house.

The space was a small room, really a confluence of four hallways that converged but the doorways were off center. The walls were painted a creamy yellow. Original artwork hung by strings looped around hooks on the bright white crown molding. His mother rotated pieces often through this small gallery.

Danny flipped on the light switch and stood in front of a new piece of artwork: a 3-D painting and sculpture. A colorful landscape was dominated by a pond. Dark blue and red branches lining the pond projected an inch or so off the canvas. He had never seen art like this and it was very engaging. The other walls displayed more traditional impressionistic oils painted by local artists.

He exited the gallery and sidestepped his way slowly through the crowd to the kitchen. As he hoped, his mother was there which spared him snaking his way through the crowded house looking for her. She initiated a hug and a kiss on the cheek.

After repeating Thanksgiving wishes, Janice asked Danny about the Ninth Street Merchants Christmas party a month from now.

"I'm so glad that we could get your quartet for the party, Danny. Have you been practicing regularly?" What Danny used to see as nagging he now accepted as motherly-advice.

"Oh, yes. That reminds me, I need to put this wine down at the drinks station," he lifted the bag of wine bottles and left before the details of his practice schedule were examined and, ultimately, rejected as 'regular practice'.

Danny made his way through the throng towards the wine table. As he approached, another guest was distributing his homemade baklava on a silver tray. Danny took one and, remembering how good they were last year, reached for another. "Don't be so greedy!" said the ersatz waiter as he maneuvered the tray away from Danny's grasp.

When Danny returned to the kitchen, peering hopefully for an unattended tray of baklava, his mother was in a heated discussion with Tammy Rose. Danny was friends with the ice cream store owner, so he was going to crack a joke, but he steered away from them as he could tell their conversation was becoming more emotional.

Tammy was mad about something and Janice was neither agreeing nor disagreeing, but trying to calm Tammy down. Danny moved closer to his mother, with his back turned, but he could still overhear.

Tammy said tightly, "What was he doing at the Leslie's Lounge, then, if he wasn't following me?" She folded her arms tightly over her chest.

Janice used her motherly voice to try to calm Tammy down. "You're letting your imagination get away from you. You think he was 'following' you at that club because you feel guilty about the way you're treating Allie."

Janice lowered her voice and put her hand on Tammy's shoulder. "Besides, I thought you were involved with someone else now. I thought you were over her, it's been almost a year. And you two were always breaking up, over and over. Wasn't it you that always said that the community is here for any woman who wants it? That's what's most important, not whether Allie wants it or doesn't want it now. Or ever. Allie can do what she wants."

Tammy paused, but would not be deterred. "That's not the point. She's making a horrible decision. When she comes running back there might not be anyone who wants to be her friend. The same might be true for you, Janice, you two-faced... ahhh!" she finished with a guttural slur.

Tammy walked away from Janice's hand and grabbed a napkin to wipe her tears. She stormed off, pushing her way through the crowd. Janice looked down for a moment or two and then followed her.

Ten minutes later, Janice returned to the kitchen and gave Danny a shoulder hug. "I'm sorry you had to hear that. This party isn't the place for her to air out her problems."

Danny shrugged slightly and puckered his lips into an understanding line, scrunching up his cheek a little on the left side of his mouth. He was mad at Tammy for talking to his mother like that, but he would let it pass if that's what his mother wanted.

"That's OK. You should have seen what happened to me at Dad's last party. Glenn and I got cornered with Dad and he launched into his theories/visions of the creation of the universe[1]. For *fifteen* minutes."

---

[1] *Space and time dimensions interact to* induce *the creation of discrete four dimensional bubbles called space-time quanta that have physical properties including randomly fluxing energy fields and maximum energy state levels.*

There is such a thing as three dimensions of space (height, width, depth) that tightly interact together as a unit. The value of the three dimensional state, when interacting with other dimensions, can range from near zero to infinity. When not interacting, the three dimensional state has a *null* value.

There is such a thing as one dimensional time. The time dimension points in a particular direction, which we call 'forward'. The time dimension must interact with space dimensions for the direction of time to manifest itself. The value of time, when interacting with space dimensions, can range from near zero to infinity. When not interacting, the one dimensional time state has a *null* value.

There is such a thing as *induction* between the space and time dimensions that *creates* quantum space-time bubbles with physical properties. When the closely-bound three dimensions of space interact with the time dimension, they *induce* into *existence* a four dimensional space-time quantum bubble.

The first four dimensional space-time quantum bubble created led to our universe.

The primordial four dimensional space-time quantum bubble was not *bigger* than anything, not *smaller* than anything, not *older* or *younger* than anything - it was not the *same as* or *different than* anything. There was only the *one* quantum bubble. There was no relativity - there was nothing for the primordial quantum bubble to be relative *to*.

A property of a space-time quantum bubble is that energy states randomly flux through it.

Space-time quantum bubbles have physical properties. One property is that energy fields flux through the space-time quantum bubble. The energy fields flux between states with very small to very large values, perhaps also with a property of being "negative" or "positive" energy.

A basic property of a space-time quantum is that there is a maximum level energy state that is sustainable (i.e., a maximum energy density). When that level is exceeded, the quantum bubble rips and creates new quanta and transfers excess energy to the new quanta. Some energy is lost is the ripping of the bubble and in the generation of the new space-time quantum bubbles. This energy loss is an expression of the fundamental laws of conservation and entropy in the space-time universe.

At some point, an energy state fluxed through the primordial quantum bubble. This particular energy state was nearly infinite "positive" energy and nearly zero "negative" energy. This particular high energy flux state was as real and valid as any other energy state that had randomly fluxed through the primordial space-time quantum bubble. However, this particular energy state exceeded the maximum energy density that a quantum bubble can withstand. Thus, the bubble burst, ejecting sticky quantum space-time bubbles to absorb the excess energy.

This "bursting" of the primordial space-time quantum bubble was the Big Bang.

This ejection new quantum space-time bubbles was the beginning of our universe. Once there were *two* space-time bubbles, *that* was the beginning of everything in our universe: measurable space, measurable time, measurable energy - relativity began because now there was something for the primordial space-time quantum bubble to be relative *to*.

Janice smiled from experience and asked "Pre-Big Bang or Post-Big Bang?"

"Don't laugh, Mom. Fifteen minutes is longer than you think."

She laughed again. "So, Danny, are you looking forward to playing for the Christmas Party? It's coming up quick so I hope you're practicing!" Danny indulged her again with a smile; it was unusual for his mother to repeat herself like that. She must be more upset than she looks, he thought.

"We're having a rehearsal next Saturday so we'll be ready to go. Any special requests?"

His mother "Remember that song you did here last year of, of... how does it go ....'right down Santa Claus Lane'?"

Danny nodded. "'Here Comes Santa Claus'. OK, I'll put it on the play list."

These new bubbles were spit out of the primordial quantum bubble like soap bubbles from a child's bubble pipe, each new bubble containing near the maximum amount of energy possible. The newly created space-time bubbles are sticky and stick to each other; that's why space-time looks continuous to us, except when you get down to the 10^{-35} m range.

The party continued on until nearly midnight. Danny stayed the night in the guest room (his old room) so that he could help clean up in the morning. As he lay in bed, he could hear sporadic gentle sobs interspersed in the murmurs of his mother and Tammy talking downstairs.

Chapter 14 - December 1

Alexandria was slightly annoyed. First, she wasn't that good with directions and she had never been to Hay Valley before. Second, her GPS hadn't' been working lately and it couldn't even tell her how to get to I-40 from her house. Third, she was ambivalent about meeting Tammy.

Tammy had texted Alexandria and asked her to meet her for a Friday afternoon drink at the Hay Valley strip mall off 15-501 headed south from Chapel Hill. The strip mall was made of concrete and looked about as unappealing as possible, Alexandria thought as she pulled in, especially in the dim December daylight. She realized now that she had passed it several times without notice over the years but its prosaic appearance never piqued her interest.

As she walked from her car into the main building, Alexandria could see that the neighborhood was in for an upgrade – a Walmart was under construction about a mile down the road.

Alexandria walked through a door into a courtyard which was entirely concealed from the road and the parking lot. What looked from the outside to be bushes in pots on the wall turned out to be a large stand of bamboo which peeked over the wall. The courtyard was much larger than it looked from the outside and contained several small buildings. A few groups of two to three people sat in each building eating, talking, drinking. As Alexandria meandered through the courtyard, she saw the source of the drinks: a small bar nestled in one corner of the courtyard.

At the bar, Alexandria turned around to look for Tammy again, and not seeing her, ordered a glass of red wine. She took her glass of wine and napkin out into the courtyard again and followed a stone path that led behind one of the stands of bamboo. Six or seven tables with chairs and umbrellas were placed on the small pebble stoned yard. Along the back of the courtyard wall were three - 'cabanas' was the best description that Alexandria could think of – three cabanas in a row. Each cabana was about ten feet wide and five feet deep and had two chairs, a small glass table, a patio couch, and a door/drape that looked a lot like a shower curtain. All three were empty and Alexandria wandered into the far corner. When she turned around, Tammy was suddenly right in front of her.

"Jesus, you scared me Tammy!" She put one hand to her chest and tried to steady her wine with the other.

Tammy smiled and took advantage of the sudden energy by standing on her toes and kissing Alexandria before she could protest.

She put her heels down and gave one of her big smiles. "We can stay in this one - I had it reserved."

Alexandria put on a grin and sat down. She took a sip of wine and leaned back in the chair.

Tammy closed the drape and sat down on the sofa, picking up her glass of wine.

Tammy lifted her glass and said with a smile, "Happy Friday, Allie!"

Alexandria lifted her glass in response. "How did you find out about this place? It's gorgeous. Look at all that bamboo. And so many birds."

The eight feet tall cabana was made of reinforced aluminum poles walled with thick canvas. Being the end cabana, two sides were surrounded by thick stands of bamboo. A third side shared a wall with the empty middle cabana. The closed drapes blocked the view of the front patio.

"Janice used to come here when she was a grad student at UNC," Tammy answered. "It was more of an artists colony; lots of paintings and sculptures back then. But they definitely had some rooms like this back in the day, she told me."

Alexandria sipped her wine and began to relax. It was a beautiful late afternoon and the only sound was the low rumble of occasional traffic on 15-501. A few clouds hid the pale new moon traversing, oblivious to those who believed the moon only came out at night.

Tammy opened her purse and pulled out a cigarette. With small clippers, she cut the filter off and put it in her purse.

Then, holding the redacted cigarette between the first two fingers of her left hand, her right hand produced a lighter and clicked a flame which peaked at one inch.

"Happy Friday, Allie!" she repeated and lit the cigarette. The cigarette smelled an awful lot like marijuana to Alexandria.

Alexandria sat up and looked toward the closed drapes. "Are you crazy? Anybody could just walk by!"

Tammy exhaled through the open roof and towards the bamboo.

"There's no one around. You worry too much. Here."

She leaned towards Alexandria and held the cigarette with the burning end straight up. Alexandria sighed and took the joint and gave it a few puffs and passed it back to Tammy.

Alexandria leaned back in her chair and closed her eyes. There were several birds communicating. Four chirps. Four chirps. Five chirps. Five chirps. An airplane passed nearby. Another joint materialized and then vanished along with the wine. Tammy stood.

In a few moments, Tammy's hands were on Alexandria's shoulders, gently massaging as Alexandria's eyes opened.

"Mmmm, that feels so good." Alexandria closed her eyes again and leaned forward slightly. The hands continued to massage her shoulders, her upper back. Momentarily, Alexandria felt a kiss on the back of her neck, just below her right ear.

She jumped, startled, and stiffened. Tammy moved her massaging back to the top of Allie's shoulders.

"It's OK, Allie, it's OK."

Allie relaxed again. Tammy gently moved Allie's hair to her left shoulder and kissed her neck again. And again.

Chapter 15 – December 3

Arthur walked into his suite at AMP headquarters. His executive assistant Renae Daye met him at the door and handed him his schedule printed from Outlook.

"Good morning, Dr. Moore. You have a voicemail from Charlie Portos at H&M Venture Capital. At nine, you have a meeting with Blake Roth and Alexandria Knott. At two, you are giving your lecture on inorganic chemistry at the NC State lab."

"Thanks. Can you bring the coffee to my office?"

Renae nodded and started preparing coffee in his favorite cup: a porcelain cup and saucer set he was given in Nairobi when he keynoted a malaria conference a few years ago.

Arthur went into his office and listened to his voicemail. "Artie, this is Charlie at H&M Venture Capital. Listen, I was in a meeting with Erik Lindisfarne last night and he had a question about the monthly progress report on the Phase I/II trial. The adverse event section and abnormal labs sections seemed skimpy. He wanted me to confirm that there will be enough detail in the next report to justify the next round of funding. Gimme a call if you want to follow up. Thanks."

By 9AM, Arthur had printed out three copies of Alexandria's most recent site monitoring report which had been automatically generated by the EDC system. He read it again and then went to the conference room.

Alexandria and Blake welcomed Arthur when he entered the conference room. Arthur gave each of them a copy. They discussed the details of the report to ensure that Alexandria agreed with the computer generated summary.

Alexandria's cell phone made a loud ring and she quickly pulled her phone from her purse and fumbled it a few moments before the ringing stopped. She set it down on the table and uttered a soft apology.

When they got to the lab values section of the report, which showed no abnormal results, Alexandria stopped talking and just looked at the report quietly.

Arthur looked up and asked, "What's the matter?"

Alexandria hesitated. "I'm just not sure about this section of the report. I thought I saw a few lab results out of range on my previous visit but none showed up this time or in this report."

Blake tried to break the tension. "But surely you must be mistaken. There are so many lab values that it must be hard to remember each one."

Alexandria glanced instinctively down at her phone. She looked quickly back at Blake.

"I'm sure you're right. Otherwise there would be an indication in the database that there was an adverse event. And this" - she pointed to the report - "shows there wasn't. You're right. Okay, let's keep going."

"So you're sure?", Arthur said to finalize the topic. His blue eyes were piercing hers and she instinctively answered, "Yes," quickly.

They finished going through the report without further extended discussion regarding any point. But Alexandria's stomach was still churning after bringing up her concerns about the data. Blake reacted as he had at dinner so that was reassuring. She still had a couple of the lipstick-photo images of the lab data on her phone, but she hadn't 100% decided to show Blake.

She finally had to announce, "I'm sorry, but can we take a break for a few moments?" She quickly stood and picked up her purse.

Arthur stood and said, "I think we're done here now anyway. Thanks, Alexandria, and we'll talk to you later." Alexandria gave Blake a look that said I'll be back in a few minutes.

Arthur shook Alexandria's hand and walked her to the restrooms past the reception desk. Blake checked his email on his phone while he waited in the conference room.

A few moments later, the PA system announced, "Blake Roth to the receptionist."

Blake stood and walked briskly to the receptionist's office.

"A call for me?"

The receptionist looked down to the flashing lights and said, "Um, not any more. He hung up. But he was pretty insistent on having you paged."

"Did he say who he was?"

"He said his name was Luma," he said. "He had a slight accent, and I didn't catch his last name. He just held for a while but hung up before he left a message."

Blake made a face and said, "Oh well. Thanks," and

walked back to his office. Alexandria would take an extra few minutes when she was rattled, he had begun to learn.

In his office, Blake checked the 'missed calls' menu on his phone and the most recent one was 'private'. He looked at his email for a few minutes and then headed back to the conference room.

Alexandria re-entered the conference room a few minutes before Blake. She sat down and saw her phone under her report. She clutched at her purse and realized that she had taken the phone out when it rang during the meeting. When she tapped the top button, the phone came alive without a password screen. Her heart dropped – she always kept her phone locked but maybe she unlocked it while she was trying to mute the ringtones in the meeting. It was opened up to the Bluetooth screen, which she seldom used, but sometimes appeared. The Bluetooth features of the phone were still out of Alexandria's league so she never used them.

There were three new texts on her phone – they must have caused the phone to make the loud ringtones. All three were from Tammy. The blood drained from Alexandria's face. The first was a photo of Tammy and Alexandria from about ten years ago. They were at a crowded festival of some kind and they had their arms around each other as they smiled into the camera. The second was a selfie of

Alexandria and Tammy standing in front of the wine bar at Hay Valley, taken just two days ago. The third said "Love then, love now, love always". Alexandria quickly deleted the texts. She hated having her personal life intrude into her professional life, especially on her work phone. She cursed herself for meeting Tammy at Hay Valley.

She held her phone and went to the calendar. The only appointment was the Ninth St. Christmas party. Janice Wilkins had invited her and Alexandria accepted because Janice was an old friend and was the social chair. The appointment had the list of guests, caterers, the music group (she had never heard of it), the location and time. She hadn't planned on inviting Blake because there were going to be too many other people from her past around. How could he understand when she hadn't even told him about her prior relationships? And he hadn't exactly believed her about the lab data. And now with what just happened with Tammy at Hay Valley...

Her stomach started sinking – in all directions at once. She had so much to tell Blake but she couldn't seem to tell him anything.

Chapter 16 - December 7

Danny readjusted himself into the couch at Stephen's house.

"This morning I called Dr. Nygren and told him about the new email attacks on the network and Ted. I emailed him the charts from the network snooping software – that you recommended – showing how the emails came in a pattern from an IP address that led to Ted's computer. Dr. Nygren wants to meet with Ted and me tomorrow morning at 10AM. I really don't know what he's going to do, but I'll bet it doesn't end up too good for Ted. I mean, he sabotaged the network just so he could 'save the day' by stopping it – that would really boost his one-man company's resume."

"You've got to think about it in terms of a paradigm," Stephen offered to Danny with raised eyebrows. Stephen was sitting in his overstuffed chair.

Danny just shook his head slightly and muttered,

"Paradigm", and took the last swig of the Vratislav dark Czech beer he'd been nursing for the past hour.

"If this is going where I think, I need another beer first." It started even as Danny walked to the kitchen.

Stephen went into lecture mode, giving Danny 'The Professor'.

"Thomas S. Kuhn. 1962. The Structure of Scientific Revolutions, that's what 'paradigm' I'm talking about. Take the last place I worked. Please." Pause. "Nothing? Ok."

Stephen waited for Danny to sit and took a sip of beer before continuing.

"Kuhn said that a paradigm is the combination a set of acceptable ways of observing the world, of interacting with the world, and of interpreting what you learn from the world. Let's use an idea I based on Scupper, the dog we had when you were little."

Danny settled back in the couch with the comfort of his full beer. He hadn't thought about Scupper in years.

Stephen started, "I call this particular paradigm 'A Boson is Man's Best Friend.'

"Remember when we used to play 'fetch the stick' with Scupper at the park? It was clear that she considered the

113

game to be more 'keep the stick away from the master'.

"When I was far away from the stick, Scupper was content to leave the stick lying unattended on the ground. But when you or I approached the stick, she trotted closer to her prize. If I bent down to pick up the stick, she would quickly grab it and would go flying off away from me at a high speed."

Stephen took another drink from his beer bottle.

"It occurred to me that the drama unfolding with Scupper was very close to a demonstration of gauge boson theory."

Danny interrupted, standing up for his rights.

"Dad, this was supposed to be about my meeting tomorrow. Then it was supposed to be about a paradigm. Now it's about God knows what, a bozo theory. Come on."

Stephen quickly corrected him.

"That's boson theory, not bozo theory. Now just listen.

"A boson transmits a force in the universe. Like a photon that transmits the electromagnetic force, let's say that Scupper is a boson transmitting a force that acts on the stick. It's easier to imagine if Scupper is invisible."

Danny almost choked on his beer.

"Now that we can't see Scupper, the scene unfolds this way for you and me. We are in the park, looking at a large stick lying in the grass. I notice that as I approach the stick, it remains stable and unmoving. But as soon as I get within one foot of it, about to take possession of the stick, it flies off at high speed in a random direction away from me - as if it were being repelled by my presence. It lands far from my reach and becomes quiet and stable again. Undeterred, I approach the stick again. I walk very slowly and then as I am about two feet away from the stick, I quickly make a grab for the stick. The stick flies away even faster this time. After a few iterations of this, I give up trying to touch the stick. Within an hour of the stick laying on the grass, for no reason that I can see, the stick deteriorates and is shredded into smaller slivers."

Danny said, "Are you sure this isn't a bozo theory? I need another beer."

Stephen said, "OK, OK. Here comes the paradigm part. Let's look at the stick through the paradigm of gauge boson theory.

"Let's treat the stick as a particle. The stick particle is affected by a force called the 'Stick force'. The Stick force comes into play when another particle (me, the master, for example) gets too close to the stick. The Stick force does not like this. The Stick force will move the stick particle away from my grasp like a repulsive force. The Stick force is transmitted by the 'Scupperon' boson, our now invisible dog Scupper.

"Here comes the 'paradigm' part – how do we view and interpret what we are seeing? When observing the stick from a distance, I didn't have any effect on the stick - the Stick force is not active at this distance. But if I get close to the stick, say within one foot of the stick, all of a sudden the Scupperon appears. The Stick force is only active when another particle (me) is within one foot of the stick. The Stick force generates a Scupperon (good girl!) and the Scupperon grabs the stick and runs away from me as fast as she can. When the Scupperon gets far enough away from me, say forty feet, she drops the stick and the Stick force is no longer active. The Scupperon disappears."

"Dad," Danny asked with a worried look, furrowing his eyebrows together, "is this some kind of way of telling me what really happened to Scupper? You told me we gave her to someone with a farm so she could be happier than living in our back yard."

Stephen deflected. "Let's concentrate on the last part of the story, OK?

"Why did the stick disintegrate? After the stick lay on the grass for a while, the Scupperon boson approached the

116

stick and began chewing on it. The stick quickly disintegrated into slivers."

Stephen beamed triumphantly. "The paradigm of boson theory was the best way to observe and understand what was happening with the stick. It explained why the stick moved when I got near it, it explained why it spontaneously disintegrated."

Against his better judgment, Danny asked his dad a question.

"How exactly does this relate to Ted, again? Or the paradigm? What in the hell are you talking about?"

If Danny thought would stop his dad, he was wrong. Stephen continued enlightening his son. His son must be so thankful. Someday.

Stephen pointed his right index finger at Danny.

"Take your 'girlfriend relationship' paradigm. Not talking to me about your girlfriend is part of your girlfriend relationship paradigm. But what are acceptable activities in your girlfriend relationship paradigm? An acceptable activity would be to walk her dog together. An unacceptable activity would be for you to attend a football game together. Acceptable communication has at least three levels of indirection before the true meanings are revealed.

Unacceptable communication is a text message 'how run?'
An acceptable car would be a luxury sedan; an
unacceptable car would be a Jaguar sports car."

"Ah," said Danny, finally with something to break the
didactic moment. "A jaguar? I'd like to work that into my
paradigm."

Stephen twinkled. "On your salary, after you bought that,
you wouldn't have a pair of dimes to rub together."

"That's a long way to go for a pun, Dad, but thanks for the
pep talk," Danny said looking at the time on his phone.

Danny looked at his father seriously.

"I'm sure this is really going to help tomorrow, Dad. Thanks
a whole lot."

Stephen responded with a grin that made Danny wonder if
his dad could detect sarcasm anymore.

At 10AM the next day, Danny sat in a wooden chair in Dr.
Nygren's office. Yesterday, Dr. Nygren listened to what
Danny said and looked at the evidence gathered by the
Internet tracking software that showed that Ted was the
one behind the email virus attacks on the school. Dr.
Nygren sat behind his desk quietly.

Actually, it was his dad who had figured it out after looking at the logs of the web tracking analyzer. The email attacks came in a regular, repeating pattern that looked like a code to Stephen. There were eight attacks and there was a rough pattern of increases and decreases in the number of emails over each attack, but that was it. Danny agreed that there was a pattern, but the code part was a bit farfetched.

Danny mentioned the pattern, but not the code conspiracy, when showing the reports to Dr. Nygren. After asking a few questions, Dr. Nygren silently accepted the conclusion and had scheduled this meeting for today, even though it was a Saturday.

Danny was very uncomfortable thinking about the conflict that would come up in the meeting with Ted. In order to take his mind off the emotions of the situation, Danny started analyzing the upcoming meeting in terms of a paradigm, like his father had prattled on about last night.

What was the paradigm here? The school ran according to Quaker principles of peace, consensus, and collaboration. How would the school react to the clear evidence that Ted had arranged the email virus attacks on the school network for what Danny thought was monetary gain? If Ted could fix a virus problem, then that would add to the resume of his flagging consulting business. So if Ted was doing this for money, then he should surely be fired, even if Ted's father was a big contributor to the school.

Paradigm question: how does a principal of the school deal with this conflict of interest?

Ted came into the office and sat down next to Danny with a short hello to Danny which was returned with a nod and a silently mouthed 'hello'.

Dr. Nygren kept his hands folded on his desk while he laid it out with an authoritative but fair voice.

"Ted, I know that you are responsible for the email virus attack on the DFS network."

Ted didn't say anything but started to turn red with embarrassment. Danny was feeling uncomfortable, too. Dr. Nygren let the moment develop in silence with the emotions churning.

Danny wondered what Dr. Nygren was feeling while he sat calmly looking at Ted.

Paradigm answer one: Dr. Nygren didn't waste time and create more embarrassment by asking Ted if he did it, saving them all the discomfort of denials before an ultimate confession.

Finally, Ted said, "I'm sorry" and continued to look at the floor.

Dr. Nygren's voice turned very soft and reassuring. "Some

people might think you did this for money, to make your consulting company prosper, Ted, but I know that's not true, is it?" Dr. Nygren looked gently at Ted.

Paradigm answer two: Follow the money. Dr. Nygren was going to let Ted off the hook because of his father's contributions that the school desperately needed. Danny let out a small silent sigh.

"That's not why you did it, Ted, is it?"

A small shake of the head as Ted continued to look at the floor.

Dr. Nygren continued softly.

"It was the pattern, wasn't it? Your pattern? I saw the pattern you made with the emails."

Danny looked up at Dr. Nygren. Yes, there was a pattern, but it you could only see it in the bar charts of the frequency of emails by hour during the attacks.

Dr. Nygren continued. "There were eight attacks and the number of emails went up, then down, then up, then down, just like going up and down a musical scale in thirds. On the fourth interval, the number of emails was stayed flat for double the time of other periods. Which note was 'flat', Ted? In this last attack, which scale were you using?"

After a moment, Ted looked up from the floor and locked onto Dr. Nygren's eyes and said, "F major. I love B flat. There has to be B flat."

Danny stared at Dr. Nygren.

Dr. Nygren explained. "The fourth note in F major is B flat. That's why the number of emails in the fourth period of the email attack was 'flat' compared to the other periods." Dr. Nygren paused then continued. "When Ted was a student here, he had an …. issue that the counselors called 'structuralism'. Ted always looks for meanings not in *what* is there, but in *how* it is there. This attack on the network was not about the emails, not about money for his company, but about the pattern he could make with the emails that only he could see."

Dr. Nygren stood up to end the meeting. "Ted, you can keep working on the network here at DFS. We are your friends. But Danny will be the top administrator and the controller of the 'god' password. If you feel the urge to do this again, please come and see me first."

Danny and Ted sat for a moment until Dr. Nygren prompted them.

"That's all gentlemen," he said and added some hand waving to reinforce the idea.

Ted stood and walked out first. Danny tried to find something to say to Dr. Nygren, but the paradigm had just blown up in front of his face and he was speechless.

Chapter 17

Dear Annie,

I am in love with a man, let's call him 'Blake'. We've been
together almost eight months now but I haven't been able
to tell him about my past. He hasn't asked, and I haven't
offered. A few weeks ago, I met a former girlfriend (yes,
that's one of the things I haven't told him) for a drink and
things got a little out of hand and I made a mistake. A
mistake, a one-time relapse into our old relationship, I don't
know what to call it.

'Blake' and I have some issues at work; he doesn't trust my
technical opinion and that makes me mad at him. But I
don't see how I can confront him for not trusting me when
I'm not trusting him enough to tell him about my past.

I'm planning on telling him everything this weekend. But
what if I really do care for my old girlfriend? Am I making a
mistake by telling him these things too soon? Or should I

just wait and hope he breaks up with me?

Signed,

Equipositional

Dear Equipositional,

It seems to me like you have no real complaints. You need to tell 'Blake' everything – you are who you are and that's it! So take my advice – stop wishing for bad luck and take control of your life.

Signed,

Dear Annie

December 18 – The Corey Coiler Show

"Today, on the Corey Coiler Show, meet men whose girlfriends have something in common with them - other girlfriends! First let's bring out Blake."

The audience applauded politely as Blake walked onto the stage and sat in the first of four barstools.

"Blake," Corey said while looking at an index card in his hand, "tell us a little about your predicament."

Before Blake could reply, Corey smiled and said, "Well, pre-*dick*-ament may not have been the best choice of words. Sorry."

"Co-rey! Co-rey! Co-rey!" from the audience in appreciation.

Blake started out slowly. "Well, Corey, my girlfriend and I had been going out for about eight months. We'd been getting along quite well, especially in the bedroom, until about a month or so ago."

"What happened then?" Corey inquired with a quizzical expression as he walked amongst the audience.

"First, we started having some work problems. She said I didn't trust her but I knew she had to be mistaken - those computer systems don't make mistakes. Then about two weeks ago she became really distant, and finally she asked me to come to her house this weekend to talk about it. Bottom line, a couple of weeks ago, she had had a fling with an old girlfriend."

Boos from the audience in sympathy.

"Tell me about it," Blake said to the audience. "I mean, she hadn't even told me about her past. I was really serious about her, you know? But then to be told that she was flinging with her old girlfriend, well I was offended I mean, I guess I'm not good enough for her in bed. I wasn't even good enough for her to tell me about her past until now."

More boos from the audience.

"I don't know what to think now. Apparently, my girlfriend and her ex had seen each other on and off for years. They would break up, sow their wild oats, and then get back together again. But this time I got in the way of their usual reunion."

Corey asked sympathetically into the microphone, "What did you do when she told you?"

Blake turned a little red. Finally, he answered, "I told her I didn't want to see her anymore and then I walked out. It's been just a few days, but I haven't talked to her since. I'm not sure that's how I really feel, but that's what I had to say then."

Polite applause from the audience.

Corey faced the camera. "Back in a moment with more losers."

Chapter 18 – December 21

Danny felt the sound of his drums bouncing off the timber supports of the large ballroom. The Ninth Street Merchants Association Christmas party was being held at the Wisco, a converted tobacco warehouse that now hosted functions, a little on the wrong side of the tracks and at a little better price than was available elsewhere in Durham. The room was huge, with two foot diameter hundred year old posts holding up the roof ornately, distinctively, and effectively. On most Friday and Saturday nights, it was 'The Wisco Disco', with the owner doubling as a bad ass DJ from Milwaukee. On nights like this, the Wisco was hosting the Ninth Street Merchants Association Christmas Party.

The band was setting up in the far right corner of the room. About a dozen service people in black shoes, black pants, white shirts, and black ties (Windsor knots for the men and bow ties for the women) were distributing hors d'oeurves to the early arrivers at the party and setting up buffet tables.

Another six servers were stationed behind strategically placed bars doing a brisk open bar business. Danny had the drum kit assembled and the rest of the band was not far behind. Bob and Christina had arrived a few minutes late and they were continuing their set up.

Danny got off the throne and walked over to them and said, "So, how are the newlyweds? Still deciding which is more important, the keyboards or the bass?" Christina was as dressed up as she got, wearing black pants and a red blouse that went well with her black hair. Her eyes were as green as Danny's.

As always, her smile dominated her face when she replied, "The bass is more important, of course! But we still need the keyboards." She chuckled and Bob smiled in a way that showed that their 'in loveness' allowed him to interpret all her comments as friendly.

Bob was an inch or so shorter than Christina and had the well-tuned body of a weight lifter. "Quit being such a bassist!", he joked back to her. They all laughed.

Bob followed with, "Let's get set up." The pre-game joking over, Bob and Christina spent the next few minutes tuning her bass to his keyboards.

Danny walked over to Glenn and whispered to him, "Do you think their marriage is going to stick?" Glenn, who at sixty five was a cool forty years older than Danny and about as cynical as Stephen, joked quietly to Danny, "I don't know if it's going to stick, man, but it sure is gonna leave a mark."

Danny laughed and then sat down on the throne. He closed his eyes and visualized his performance. The hum of people talking in the 'audience' was beginning to build. The clink of empty glasses being bused into plastic tubs was especially nice. Christina rustled bass sheet music into the proper order and was singing softly to herself. Glenn was tapping the keys of his Selmer Mark VI tenor saxophone. The drone of the audience built and merged with the warm-up sounds of the band.

Danny hit the snare drum – everyone in the room could hear it. That was a sense of musical power that always struck him – he was in control of the music that filled the room. As always, he hoped the audience would enjoy the music, but not everyone was a jazz/blues fan. This dashed hope was usually followed by the realization that his musical expression ultimately mattered more to him than the approval of semi-listening, semi-inebriated audiences. The music felt beautiful and filled him with confidence. Bang the snare drum again.

Two servers chatted briefly near the band, talking about the new members on the serving crew and the troubles they were causing. The servers were at the party to make a living, not to listen to music or party with friends – that made them akin to the band.

Glenn nodded to Danny and the music began. His bass drum and hi hat set the exact tempo of the song. A fraction faster or slower would also have done, but Danny laid it down like he heard it in his head. As he worked through the changes, laying the path for the sax and bass, he leaned into the beats as he liked. Tonight, he focused on taking the hi-hat from crisp hits to long vibrations. The sax broke into its solo and Glenn leaned into notes to echo the pattern of Danny's beat. This created an intimacy between the musicians that was easy during the performance and understandably disappeared with the last note of each song.

The audience managed to suppress applause in between the first few songs – perhaps they were 'saving their applause for the end'. At eight o'clock, Janice, wearing a red dress, walked up to microphone and waited for the song to end. Danny hadn't noticed her waiting with her hands folded in front of her and her public smile on. During songs, his eyes alternated from being closed to staring off to the side. The song ended and the first applause came.

Janice applauded and said, "Thank you. Thank you very much. The 'Tan Moviles Quartet', everybody." Danny nodded and smiled at the audience in appreciation and then slouched on his throne.

Janice turned and addressed the crowd of approximately 100 guests.

"Welcome everyone to the Ninth Street Merchants Association Christmas Party. My name is Janice Wilkins and I am this year's social chair. One of the perks is to host the Christmas Party. And to pick the band." She turned and gave Danny a big smile which he returned. "Let's have another big round of applause for 'The Tan Moviles Quartet'." The audience clapped and the band bowed to the audience, basked in their ten seconds of glory, and then turned their attention again to Janice.

"Tonight we are having an open bar," she continued. The crowd broke into loud applause and shouts of appreciation. She turned to the right and said to someone at the table in front of her, "What?" Returning back to the audience she said, "Sorry, I was just told that the open bar just ended at 8PM." Mock 'boos' came from the audience. She laughed and held both hands up and said, "Beer and wine are still available for $5 each."

She assumed the clasped hands and public smile again. "The buffet will start in a few moments. We will be having fish, chicken cordon bleu, and plenty of vegetarian dishes from Vine. Desserts will be provided by Tammy Rose and 'Renata's'. I hope everyone has a wonderful evening." The crowd applauded and Janice walked over to Danny.

"Thanks for playing tonight, sweetie." She smiled and gave him a kiss on the cheek. She then thanked Christina, Bob, and Glenn and walked off the stage.

Glenn called out a tune and Danny tapped his sticks to set the beat. Christmas jazz filled the room.

The last song before the break was 'Here Comes Santa Claus', Janice's special request.

When the band took its break some fifteen minutes later, Danny put on his Christmas music CD and plugged it into the PA system. 'Santa Baby' by Eartha Kitt was the lead.

Danny spotted Janice at a large round table, walked over with his food, and sat down. Janice introduced him to the group, including Alexandria Knott. Danny was a course behind the rest of the group which was finishing dinner and most were looking around for the dessert.

Danny ate his dinner a little self consciously. A shaggy haired waiter placed a bowl of ice cream in front of everyone's plate. Danny shook his head "No, thanks" when offered his choice of ice cream.

Alexandria's ice cream was in a small tupperware container

with a note on the lid. The waiter placed a bowl next to the container in front of Alexandria's place. She opened the note – "A - Merry Christmas – Love, T", crumpled it, and put it in her purse. She said thank you to the waiter, emptied the ice cream into the bowl, and ate a large spoonful.

Danny remembered a joke his father told him and decided to try it out here. He said, "The waiter put my water on the left side. How gauche." It got a few laughs from the French speaking crowd; Danny made a mental note to thank his dad.

A different waiter came by a few minutes later and removed the ice cream bowls. Alexandria started to say Thank You but be she couldn't speak. She started clutching at her throat and began to choke. A man sitting next to Danny got up quickly and gave the Heimlich maneuver but there didn't seem to be anything stuck in her throat. A few moments later, Alexandria passed out and they laid her on the floor. Janice yelled for someone to call 911.

Chapter 19 - December 22 Durham Morning Herald

Woman Poisoned at Ninth Street Merchants Association Party

A woman poisoned at the Ninth Street Merchants Association Christmas Party last night is unconscious at Duke Hospital. Durham Police Department Detective Sergeant Louis Roberts confirmed that Alexandria Knott, 35, of Durham, was poisoned with arsenic in ice cream at approximately 10PM last night. Police have a suspect in custody. Tammy Rose, 35 and also of Durham, and owner of "Renata's Ice Cream" on Ninth Street, was arrested at the scene based on eyewitness accounts of her involvement with the assault.

Chapter 20 – December 27

The fifteen minute drive from his mother's house to his father's house stretched into a half hour as Danny drove slowly through the ice and rain. The Spider buffeted from side to side as wind gusts pushed at the sports car. A few slides as the car lost traction convinced Danny to slow down even more as he entered his father's neighborhood.

There was ice on Stephen's driveway so Danny parked on the street and jogged up the lawn through the bitter cold wind. Stephen quickly opened the door and Danny hopped into the house.

Hoping to head off the inevitable poem, Danny threw a movie line at his dad. "'It's fricking freezing out there, Mr. Bigglesworth.' That wind is brutal Dad." But Stephen was undeterred and let loose with "'One must have a mind of winter, and have been cold a long time not to think of any misery in the sound of the wind...'" but Danny was already taking off his jacket and scarf so he didn't hear the end.

Danny dropped his small overnight bag in the guest room, got a beer from the kitchen, and collapsed onto the couch. They were headed for a ski trip tomorrow after his gig.

"So, Dad, what's up with the junk email art exhibit? Any progress?"

Stephen swiveled the computer chair towards Danny and answered as if it had been a serious question.

"I had to put that aside for a while, though I'm glad to hear that you are interested. I'm showing it at the users group in a few weeks. No, I'm working on the updated member list for the data manager's users group. When we get back from skiing, I'll have to post the updated list to the website."

After a few minutes of silence and a few pulls of beer, Danny wandered over to where his dad was sitting and looked over his shoulder. Stephen was scrolling through the list of names and something caught Danny's eye.

"Hey Dad, wait a minute, go back a page." Stephen stopped and scrolled back one page. Danny said, "No, one more page back."

"Here?" Stephen asked.

Danny nodded and said, "Can you print that page?"

Stephen nodded and clicked the page to the printer. The

printout was organized by company. Under the company name 'WDM, Inc.' were two entries of information: one for Alexandria Knott and one for a Merri Edwards.

Danny handed the printout to his father.

"Dad, do you know this Alexandria Knott from your users group?"

Stephen looked at the printout and tried to remember, running his left hand through his beard unconsciously. "I don't think so, but not everyone comes to the meetings. Maybe she just uses the web resources."

"Well, this is the woman who just got poisoned at the Ninth Street Christmas party I was playing at. Mom invited her."

Stephen put on a serious face. "Danny, I don't think your mother had anything to do with the poisoning."

But Danny ignored the joke and kept looking at the printout. "Don't you know anything about her?"

Stephen put on his glasses and looked more carefully at the printout. "Yeah, this company, WDM, is a fairly small monitoring company in RTP. Ok, looks like Morrisville. I heard they have a big contract on an EDC trial."

"What's EDC?"

"Electronic data capture. The idea is to capture and

manage all data electronically so that you won't have to keep updating paper copies of data, that kind of stuff. A lot of companies do that, but it is very difficult to go totally paperless."

"Do you know anything about that big contract?"

"No. But it's probably on the WDM website."

Stephen opened a Google page and typed in the website as listed on the printout and came to the WDM, Inc., main page. Under 'Clients', there were four or five company logos.

Danny tapped his father on the shoulder, so Stephen stood up and Danny sat down in front of the monitor. He clicked on the first company and Stephen said, "Why don't you do that when we come back from skiing?"

Danny's phone rang; the crickets ringtone meant that it was his mother.

Danny put the call on speaker. "Hi Mom, I'm at Dad's. You're on speaker."

She started, "Danny, the decorator wants to know what kind of countertop I should put in, but you're better at these things. I have to get the order placed by New Year's so I need your help." Even over the iPhone speaker, Stephen could hear the love in her voice when she talked with their son. She asked, "Should I get Italian marble, yellow limestone, Brazilian granite, artificial granite, or what?"

Danny thought and said, "I think you'd like the Italian marble. I've never heard of the yellow limestone but it sounds cool."

Stephen offered his unsolicited opinion towards the iPhone. "Au contraire, mon frer, I think she would like the Brazilian granite better."

After a moment of silence, Janice finally spoke. "Actually, the decorator left several samples and I'd have to say that I really do like the Brazilian granite."

Stephen beamed to Danny, and composed his voice in a way that Danny know only spelled trouble.

"See Danny? I told you she always took my opinions for granite."

After a long pause, Janice replied, "That one hurt, even over the phone."

Chapter 21 – December 29

Danny woke to the smell of fresh coffee. Moments later burning bacon followed. He rolled over and looked out the window. He gazed at the pine trees covered with snow. A row of junipers sagged with thick ice. The far off firs reflected the sunrise.

The cabin in the Catskills was rustic and satisfying. Yesterday, Stephen and Danny left Durham after Danny's last drumming gig of the holiday. The trip was a welcome diversion from the attempted murder and the anguish it was causing Janice. They would fly back to Durham on New Year's Day – this morning was nestled cozily at the start of the vacation.

Danny considered taking his shower. His father put the 'hour' in 'shower'. But he donned his snow clothes and stepped outside. Thick snow fell effortlessly in silence. An unseen creek rushed over smooth boulders. Danny listened for birds, but heard nothing. He could see his father cooking breakfast. A perfect snowball took shape in his hands. It launched of its own accord at the house. His dad looked up as it hit the window. He held up two cooked pieces of bacon. Danny stared as the bacon disappeared. The snowball was worth his bacon ration.

His father served breakfast, and made peace by giving Danny the two remaining pieces of bacon. After cleaning the kitchen, they packed for the short trip to the ski lodge.

The car warmed quickly, too quickly for Danny, who was dressed in several layers of ski clothes. Danny won the music contest by starting Amy Winehouse's 'Rehab' before his dad could insist on more traditional jazz. 'They tried to make me go to rehab, but I won't go go go.' It was only ten minutes to the lodge, even with the snow. They parked, rented the equipment (Danny's treat, Stephen had picked up the other expenses), and walked into the lodge area.

Inside the lodge, Danny noticed the way the ski-booted skiers duck-walked across the slick rubber floor. Some looked as if they were riding a horse, bobbing up and down with a bow-legged gait. The rubber floor was no doubt efficient considering the melting snow but it was quite ugly. Danny parked his father near the window and went to get two cups of hot chocolate.

The ski lodge was built of dark brown planks that formed a low peak. The center of the lodge was dominated by a large red metallic fireplace that tapered up to the roof with the final ten feet narrowing to a chimney. The room was crowded with large circular tables orbited by peripatetic folding chairs.

This place reminded Stephen of when he was young and his parents took him to a lodge with a similar fireplace. It was at Arrowhead Lake in the San Gabriel mountains near Los Angeles. The Arrowhead Lodge had an A frame that was more pronounced than this, but similar. There had been bear heads mounted on the wall.

Stephen looked down at his left palm and remembered. While waiting in the Arrowhead Lake lodge, the eight year old Stephen had ever so nonchalantly leaned against the fireplace, placing his bare hand on the hot surface. It made a severe burn and he cried steadily for minutes. He felt foolish for doing something so stupid and even more foolish for crying in front of his parents.

As he whimpered, Stephen's mother comforted him and held a bag of ice to his hand. The pain throbbed and would not stop. When Stephen had composed himself, they left the lodge and rented a canoe to paddle on Arrowhead Lake. His father rowed and Stephen leaned against his mother while he dragged his burned hand through the cold water to kill the pain.

Danny returned with a cup of hot chocolate in each hand to find his father in reverie, staring at his left hand. What was he thinking? Was he thinking about the ring that was no longer on his left ring finger?

His father accepted the cup of hot chocolate with his left hand and felt the warmth as he peeked under the lid. No whipped cream.

At this point, Danny no longer felt the disappointment in his stomach when he thought of his parents' divorce. Stephen jokingly described it as an amicable split – 'I was amicable and she split.' Danny's childhood dream that his parents would reunite had long ago given way to the satisfying reality that his parents got along and loved each other on a dimension far from daily living.

Stephen looked directly at Danny. "Let me give you some fatherly advice about long-term relationships, my son."

"I'm sorry, did I ask?" Danny tried to deflect.

Stephen took that time to compose himself.

"You both must decide which path to believe:

Details that destroy or feelings that bloom.

If feelings you choose, the details must leave;

If details you choose, 'tis your love you doom."

They finished their drinks in silence. A few minutes later, sporting chocolate mustaches with no whip cream, Danny and his father walked out into the cold towards the ski lift.

Chapter 22 – January 3

Danny drove to his mother's house to see her for New Year's, even though it was a few days after. As Danny was parking in the driveway, he saw Tammy Rose's classic orange/white VW microbus with a 'Renata's Ice Cream' bumper sticker. The catering bus looked like an orange creamcicle. Danny hadn't heard that Tammy was out on bail.

After the hellos, Janice asked Danny about the ski weekend with his dad. Danny said that Stephen was strangely subdued, reflective on his life. Janice said that she was glad that everything went so well on the trip.

Danny leaned on the new Brazilian counter tops and voiced his appreciation.

Tammy was sitting to the side, looking a little weepy, and Danny felt like he had interrupted another high drama conversation though this one was understandable.

Janice told him that her friend Diana Virbius from WDM, Inc, who was a regular at the book readings at Helena's, had called her and asked if Danny could come to the office and help with a network problem. Something about file permissions of Alexandria Knott and the other staff needed access. Even though it was still vacation, he didn't feel like he could say no in the current atmosphere. Besides, he had just seen Alexandria's name on his dad's mailing list.

Danny's iPhone chirped in his pocket. He gave it a quick look and saw a series of emails from his Internet snooping program alerting him about another problem at the school's server. He got up to leave and said he would stop by WDM on his way home from the school.

Chapter 23 – January 3

Danny drove the Spider into the empty parking lot at DFS. Spending Friday morning at school on an off day was not exactly what he had planned, but his mother's request that he give some IT help to her friend's company (the one where the company leader was poisoned at the Christmas party) had already turned this into a work day. The clincher was that the Internet snooping software he installed just sent him a message that the server needed to be rebooted. He wanted to make sure he did it before Ted tried to butt in.

To make up for his inconvenience, Danny parked the Spider in the principal's parking spot. Dr. Nygren wouldn't like seeing that, to say nothing of Mrs. Carson, but that was half the fun. He deserved *something* for spending his last day of vacation at the school.

Danny went to his desk and rebooted the server. While the computer was resuscitating, Danny made a pot of coffee just the way he liked it: three packets of coffee. No one there to complain. Danny flashed back to the film noir movies that his father made him watch growing up. Ingrid Bergman making coffee with 'an egg' in 'Spellbound'. He asked his dad what kind of egg goes in coffee. His dad had responded, "Scrambled" and that had the young Danny thinking for quite a while.

But first things first. Danny fired up the network snooping program to see if there had been any attacks on the DFS network. After Dr. Nygren had given Danny control over the network, Danny had been able to track and block most legitimate attacks using the Internet snooping software his dad recommended. The logs over the last few days were clean of attacks, but the school had been closed so perhaps that was part of the reason. There was a series of attacks last night, but it didn't look like Ted's handiwork and the network firewall had handled it.

Convinced that the network was not in any danger, Danny turned his attention to the company he was supposed to help in a few hours. He googled the woman who was poisoned, Alexandria Knott, and quickly came to WDM Inc.'s website. He hadn't gotten around to researching all their clients, as he had started to do before the ski trip.

With the touch of a key, the Internet snooping software showed the HTML that ran the website. 'Celise Designs' was the webmaster and the site hadn't been updated in a few months. The software pointed to the only data entry interface on the website: a screen for prospective clients to request more information. That type of data entry screen was an easy target for hackers to inject code into the website to perform whatever nefarious tasks the hackers performed.

He looked through the 'Who are we' pages and saw pictures of the WDM staff. The poisoned woman was the CEO. The senior monitor he recognized as Diana Virbius, the name of his mother's friend. He recognized her from several readings at his mother's book store. The page listed the other staff of clinical research monitors. The only other name he recognized was Merri Edwards, who was listed on his dad's data management user group's membership list. The WDM office was located near RTP, a few miles from his coffee hangout The Savvy Café.

The 'Clients' page had three company logos. Danny clicked on each one and followed the links. He had heard of two of the companies, GSK and Merck, but not the third, AMP. After a few clicks, it was clear that WDM must have been working with AMP on a new HIV vaccine.

After double checking that the network server was OK, Danny locked the server keyboard and headed to WDM to help with their network problems.

Danny asked for Diana Virbius at the receptionist's desk and soon she had taken him into her office and he was logged into her computer. It would have been better to work on Alexandria's computer, Diana told him, but the police had confiscated it as part of the investigation after they were unable to locate her cell phone. Diana explained that his main task was to give her access to Alexandria's network folders.

Diana said gratefully, "Thanks so much for coming in on such short notice. We usually get IT help from the office down the hall but they don't come back until Monday. Everyone here is still in shock about Alexandria and we really need to get access to her study files on the network, but nobody can access them or knows how to fix the problem."

Danny said, "No problem, I am happy to help. Do you have the administrator username and password?"

Diana handed him an index card. "Here is what the other IT guys gave us for that. I've never used it but it should work." Diana fed her hamster and replaced the water while she waited for Danny to ask her which folders needed permission modifications.

A few minutes later, there was a loud commotion at the receptionist's desk. Diana left to see what the problem was. As the commotion continued, Danny stuck his head out the door to see what was going on.

A well-dressed, important looking man was at the receptionist's desk loudly demanding that he be given copies of all of Ms. Knott's files for his study. He was tall and bald and he was, as he pointed out several times, Arthur Moore, CEO of AMP, a very important client to this company. The receptionist was trying to tell him that that wasn't possible, but Arthur Moore who didn't take no for an answer. Diana told him that that wasn't possible now but she would call him when it was. After a few more minutes of demanding, he stormed out of the office with threats about his lawyers.

Diana returned to the Alexandria's office and sighed. "Sorry about that, Danny. Where were we?"

Danny replied, "I just need you to tell me who needs access to which folders. Where did – does – she keep the files?"

Belinda said, "All the files under the 'projects' folder for 'AMP HIV003'. I need access, and so does the primary monitor on the AMP study. That is Merri Edwards. She should know if anybody else needs access."

Diana walked Danny over to Merri's cube and they exchanged hellos.

"Did anyone else work closely with Alexandria on the AMP projects? Do you need access to their files?" Diana asked Merri after the introductions.

Merri thought for a moment and said, "There was a CRA before me named Vera Lynn but she left about six months ago. If it's important, I can ask the others about her."

Merri walked down a few cubes to a group of workers. "Does anybody here remember Vera Lynn?"

One of the group answered, "Was she the one who went nuclear and quit when Ms. Knott reprimanded her about not doing monitoring reports?"

Diana shook her head. "No, that was Sharon Harris. I don't think she worked on the AMP project though."

Merri said to Danny, "Well, if anyone else needs access, I can give them copies now. Thanks so much."

Danny said, "You are very welcome. I'll finish up with those permissions and then be on my way."

Chapter 24 – January 3

On the way back from WDM, Danny decided that he wanted to find out more about that jerk who had made that scene in office. He had to drive past school anyway to get home so he pulled into the parking lot and went into the server room.

When he logged into server, Danny first looked for any sign of attack on the network. There was none. Next, he googled Arthur Moore and AMP. The AMP website had several news releases that were essentially victory laps describing the last two rounds of venture capital AMP received. The most recent release had a blurb the HIV vaccine study that one Alexandria Knott was on. Had been on. Danny read the summary but he had to admit that he didn't understand several of the key words.

In the 'About Us' section of the website, Arthur Moore had a long, detailed bio. His picture showed the bald man who came into the offices shouting today. Only in this picture, he wore a smile that said he was successful and in charge. In the bio, Moore told the story of his idea for the HIV vaccine. He was working on malaria genetics and he noticed several similarities to cells reaction to HIV. Moore described his "aha!" moment when he decided to defend cells from HIV attack by using a genetic mutation that he had seen in people infected with a strain of malaria-causing *p. falciparum* parasite from Tanzania. The mutation rendered the parasite harmless to humans.

The bio went on to say that the new HIV vaccine applied these same principles and he is very hopeful that he will get similar results. The story ended with Moore saying proudly that there have been no severe adverse events reported in any of the ongoing clinical trials. The bio concluded by saying that Arthur Moore has a PhD in pharmacokinetics from the Duke University, a masters in computer science from the University of Michigan, and a bachelors in chemistry and a minor in theatre from Northwestern University. He is an adjunct professor of chemistry at NC State University.

Danny poked around some more but finally lost interest and logged into his Youtube favorites list to catch a few Shakira videos. I am a Spanish teacher, after all, he thought, just doing my job.

Chapter 25 - January 9

Arthur Moore was just finishing his review of the monthly progress report for the venture capitalists. He added a few sentences summarizing how smoothly the trial was going. There were no serious adverse events to report to the data and safety monitoring board which was meeting for the second time in the trial. Although safety labs were being analyzed, the pharmacokinetic analysis of the blood samples wouldn't be ready until a few weeks after the end of the trial.

Arthur leaned back and rubbed his eyes for a moment. The monthly telecons and reports with Erik Lindisfarne had been wearing on him, not to mention the DSMB reports. Lindisfarne was constantly warning against delays in the trial or problems with SAEs, always with a threatening undertone. And sometimes not so under.

He clicked open his copy of the data summary that had to be emailed to the DSMB today. He had barely been able to keep it out of Lindisfarne's hands. At the last telecon, Lindisfarne made it clear that the DMSB meeting results would be a key milestone in releasing the next round of capital.

Exhaling and sitting up straight, Arthur did one last spell check and then saved the monthly progress report file and emailed it to Lindisfarne. Arthur's secretary had drafted the progress report and the email. He had set up the encryption system for files he sent to H&M. He didn't trust them enough to send unprotected files – a leak could cost him millions.

He pushed back in his chair and waited.

Chapter 26 – January 12

"Hey man, what was the name of the apostle that denied Jesus three times? It was St. Peter right?"

Tut's question had Stephen thinking. 'Peter' sounded close but not with the 'Saint' – that made him think of the Pearly Gates.

"Are you sure?" Stephen asked.

Tut frowned, knitted his eyebrows together and said, "Yeah, he denied him three times at the last supper. You know, at the Olive Garden."

Danny laughed. "You know, that almost sounds right!"

While Stephen finished adding half and half to his espresso, Danny looked for their regular seat near the window. Danny had invited Merri Edwards from WDM, Inc., to meet Danny and his father at The Savvy Café. She had called him and said it was important that they meet. It was raining heavily and she hadn't arrived yet.

Stephen and Danny sat at their booth near the window and in a few minutes, Merri walked into the café. Danny stood up and walked over to greet her. She was taking off her raincoat and closing her umbrella.

"Thanks for meeting us here", Danny said. "I hope this is convenient for you."

She looked anxious but not because of me, Danny thought.

"Thanks," she said with a slight smile and a slightly sideways glance. She was wearing a white blouse and a pair of plentifully pocketed pants. She pushed wet hair behind her ears. Danny took her raincoat and umbrella and walked her to their table. Danny turned to make eye contact with Stephen, who was now standing by their table and ready to meet her.

Danny stood between them and introduced his father with a nod. "Merrimac Edwards, this is my father Stephen Yobar." She smiled and said, "Please call me Merri." They shook hands and sat down with Stephen and Merri facing each other. Danny asked Merri if she would like an espresso, and she did.

A minute later, Danny returned to the table with Merri's coffee. As Danny gave the coffee saucer and cup to her,

Danny caught a glimpse of something in his father's eyes. Surely he wasn't attracted to this woman who was twenty five years his junior, but there was a gleam.

Danny sat down and looked at Stephen.

"Merri is a clinical research associate, a clinical trials monitor, at WDM. I was helping her get access to the files of the woman who was poisoned at that Christmas party the quartet played at."

Stephen looked back to Merri, his eyes twinkled, replacing the gleam that had unsettled Danny.

He spoke clearly, "It certainly is nice to meet you, Merri. My son knows I'm a Civil War buff so I'm surprised he never mentioned you, Merrimac the monitor, to me before."

Before Danny could admonish him, Stephen leaned forward to Merri and offered an apology. "I'm sorry, Merri. It won't happen again."

Merri laughed loudly and said, "Merrimac is a Scottish name, and I've been teased before, but that's the first time I've been compared to a ship." She laughed again and then sipped her coffee to obscure her grin.

Stephen looked into her green eyes and soaked in her loud laugh.[2] Danny rolled his eyes, and briefly looked at the small painting on the wall next to their booth. The painting looked as if it were set in this coffee shop. There was a young man sitting at a table that looked just like theirs. The man in the painting was looking downward and his eyes met Danny's as he looked up.

Danny broke the scene up by saying, "Merri wanted to talk to me about some computer issue at WDM and I thought it would be great if dad" – he suppressed a grin – "Stephen – if he joined us. He knows a lot more about computers than me."

Now that the subject had been broached, she was suddenly very upset. She reached into her purse and pulled out a lipstick case with a yellow sticky note sheet stuck to it.

"This belongs to Ms. Knott, she keeps it in her office," she confessed.

---

[2] Her blue green eyes softly comfort my soul
Unabashed laughs come out in a burst
My body absorbs them and I feel whole
Peace, passion, and love all strive to be first.
Waves of beauty appear bright here and there
The longer I look the deeper I feel
My eyes and my heart have found ways to share
I see her beauty, I look but don't steal.
Although I cannot be her beloved
Merrimac is a woman to be loved.

"See, on the outside it looks like a case for one of the red lipsticks that she always wears. But it's a camera at one end with a USB connection on the other end. It was a give-away at the Drug Information Association annual meeting two years ago. I was with her when she got it from some vendor. She joked about how she could keep her secret CEO files on there."

She used her fingernail to open the hinged cover, and showed Stephen and Danny the now exposed camera lens. When she pressed the cover back on, it clicked in a very satisfactory way. The back end screwed off to expose a USB connection for a computer.

She twirled it slowly in her hands as she continued. "When Dr. Moore came over the other day demanding all our computer files, I remembered this USB. It's possible that she has something on it that she wants secret, so I didn't want Dr. Moore to get it. I know she keeps it on top of her bookcase. I feel bad for taking it but I didn't look at it or anything. I just wanted to keep her safe," she confessed again, passing the USB to Stephen.

The yellow sticky note was now on the table. She looked at it and said, "That was stuck to the lipstick case. I don't know what it means."

Danny picked up the note and read it for a few moments.

The note said 'sihdaisnegiehs'.

Stephen opened and closed the lipstick case a few times while waiting for Danny to show him the note. Danny finally passed him the note and then turned his attention back to Merri while Stephen concentrated on the note.

"Are you sure that those letters aren't somehow related to the trial you're on with Ms. Knott?" Danny followed up.

Merri's eyes looked down and to the left as she shook her head no.

"Maybe it's a password for the files", Stephen offered as he picked up the lipstick case and twirled it as Merri had.

"Well, it was an inside joke at the office that Ms. Knott liked funny passwords. She told me at the beginning of the clinical trial that she was worried about the 'all EDC' study and I thought it was possible that her 'secret CEO' lipstick case might have something on it. I figured the best thing to do was to get it out of the office so she wouldn't get in trouble. And you were working on the network files that day, so I asked Diana Virbius what to do. She said we could trust you because she knows your mother. We thought it would be best to give it to you for a while." She sounded sort of pleading at the end, trying to convince herself as much as Danny.

He took the lipstick case/camera/USB drive back from Stephen – the twirling was driving him crazy.

"We can take a look at the files on here, if there are any. My dad works in clinical trials so maybe he can figure out what is on here if it's related to the study."

Merri looked very relieved now that she wasn't in possession of the lipstick case. "Thank you so much. I really appreciate it."

She looked over her shoulder out the window and saw that it was still pouring.

"It's really bucketing out there now," she said. "I think I'll have another coffee and maybe it will have stopped by then."

She started to stand up but Danny stopped her. He said, "What would you like? I'll order it for you." She smiled - Caramel macchiato, shot of vanilla, skinny, with a double shot of espresso. He almost sat down.

Stephen copied the letters from the note onto his smart phone. He put the yellow sticky note back on the lipstick case and placed it in front of Danny's seat.

Danny walked to the bar and placed the order with Tut.

"Hey, Tut, did you see that sweet silver Porsche out there?

I parked right next to it." Danny gestured to the parking lot. The silver sports car was shining even in the rain.

Tut nodded his head, "Yeah man, it's mine."

Danny was surprised and said, "Really? What happened to your red one, man?"

"I kept it. Nothing wrong with two Porches."

Danny shook his head. "I don't know, Tut. One Porsche, that's compensating for a mid-life crisis. Two Porsches, that sounds like a plumbing problem, man."

Tut laughed and handed him the macchiato. "Shut the fuck up and give this to that pretty young lady. It looks like you guys upset her."

Chapter 27 – January 16

Stephen arrived at Durham Friends School a few minutes before he was scheduled to meet Danny. The winter sun hadn't set yet, and the clouds were so low he couldn't tell if the moon was rising. It wasn't too cold so he decided to walk down to the pond on the edge of the school grounds, where he could see Danny's car when it came. An old dinghy bobbed in the water, tied to a piling in the pond.

Stephen sat down on a bench near the edge of the pond. A few frogs were croaking. The back leg of the bench was broken but barely propped up with a brick. A huge oak, relieved of its leaves, reflected in the pond. A pair of red winged black birds commuted between the branches and bank. Wild ducks swam in groups of five or six, meandering back and forth from bank to bank. He took a deep inhale. The pond gave the impression that the whole world was peaceful. He closed his eyes, exhaled, and cleared his mind.

Breathing moved to the background. His head was levitating. Eyes still closed, cool air on his skin, the thoughts came.

Levitating brevitating hesitating meditating medicating investigating prevaricating necessitating fee-fi-fo-fum-itating resuscitating luxuritating necessessessessitating relaxitating relativitating gravitating singularitating ting ting.

He heard Danny's car approach with a rattle. With one last exhale, he stood and turned to see Danny's car parking. That boy needs a new car, he thought while walking slowly back up the hill.

Danny walked down the hill and pointed to the large heron ankling in the shallow waters of the far bank of the pond. Stephen turned and Danny stopped next to him. Danny continued slowly towards the heron. When he got to within a hundred feet or so of the bank, the heron took off with great sweeping wings. Danny followed the flight until the heron slowly arced into the tops of the tall pines.

Danny turned around and passed Stephen on the way back up the hill.

"What, no poem, Dad? Ready to go inside?" Danny continued towards the school before receiving his reply.

Stephen faced the pond and recited:

"Gray clouds softly engulf the moon
Darkness emerges from the night.
Croaks say the pond frogs will mate soon
Cool air pushes out the last light.

From bush to bush around the pond
The bullfrogs sing their ancient song
They blast their throats and look to see
A red winged black bird in his tree."

Stephen turned towards Danny but saw that his son was half-way to the school, apparently having missed the poeming. Stephen smiled though he tried not to.

He followed his son into the dingy Durham Friends School server room and sat down in the driver's seat in front of the server.

Stephen took the lipstick case and yellow sticky note out of his pocket, exposed the USB connector on the lipstick case, and inserted it into one of USB ports on the server.

The password screen came up, denying access to the files. Danny looked at his father "That's what we thought would happen. Now what?"

First Stephen typed in the letters as they appeared on the yellow sticky note. Password denied. Danny 'harrumphed' but Stephen started grinning.

He quickly typed in another long password and the USB folder opened showing a long list of files.

Danny widened his eyes and said, "Hey, how did you guess the password?"

Stephen grinned and said, "I kept thinking about these random letters written on this note. I didn't think that anyone, even someone who was good with passwords like Ms. Knott, would make a password like that. That's when I started thinking that it was an anagram. I put those letters in an anagram generator on the Internet and it came up with the phrase 'High in diseases'. I thought that was going to be the password and I was right."

Stephen sounded very proud of himself.

"Dad, you sound very proud of yourself. So what exactly is an anagram again?"

"When you rearrange the letters in a word or phrase into another word or phrase, that's an anagram."

Stephen turned his attention to the server screen which showed the USB's files, a list of about fifty image files with dates and times for their names. Stephen opened a few and after the second one, said, "These are photographs, taken from the small camera in the lipstick case. They look to be...." Stephen leaned closer to the monitor and then sat up straight.

"I was right. They're pictures of the computer screen showing case report form data from the clinical trial that Alexandria Knott was monitoring."

Danny said, "And?"

"*And* she wasn't allowed to take these pictures, remember? The lovely monitor at WDM, Merrimac, said that no one was allowed to take *any* notes on the clinical trial? The only record was *supposed* to be the EDC system that that pharma company AMP was fanatic about." Danny remembered seeing that on the AMP website when he was looking up Arthur Moore.

Stephen opened the first several files and began taking notes. He ignored Danny's questions of what are you doing.

Stephen opened five or so more of the USB files and began switching back and forth between different images. He started renaming each photo file with a code that he begrudgingly told Danny was a combination of participant identification numbers, date on the CRF, and date/time that the photo was taken. All of the photos were of laboratory safety CRFs.

Danny relented and sat down and started playing the game 2048 on his phone while his dad worked.

Stephen gave up on his hand scrawled notes and instead entered them into a table in a Word document. For the next twenty minutes he filled the Word table with data he abstracted from each photo file showing a CRF. When Stephen had filled in the last row of his table, he sorted it and printed it a few different ways.

Danny happily retrieved the printouts, finally able to contribute. He couldn't get past the 1024 level in his game anyway. His dad had that look in his eye.

Stephen announced, "Something is rotten in the state of Denmark."

"Where?" Danny asked, pointing to the printouts.

Stephen went into 'The Professor' mode again.

"OK. Each one of these photos is an image of a safety data case report form used in the HIV trial that Ms. Knott was monitoring. These case report forms are designed to identify serious adverse events and alert the study team. The lab data appears to be loaded automatically into the EDC system. I've worked on trials where we did that with a Bluetooth connection between a gas chromatograph and a router that is connected to an EDC system.

"Look at this table. Just look at the first two rows."

Stephen took a yellow highlighter and marked two values on the printout.

"These two rows show what data was in two photos on that lipstick USB drive. The photos show lab safety data case report forms for participant ID 10813. The photos are of the same lab CRF for that same date and subject ID; they should be identical. One photo was taken on August 17, and the other one was taken on October 24. But one of the lab data values is different in the two photos."

Danny didn't look quite convinced.

Stephen said, "Here, let me print the two photos. And don't use the cheap paper." Danny loaded the high quality paper and Stephen printed the photos at top resolution. Even with the school's laser printer, it took a minute to print the two photos.

Stephen laid the printed photos down next to each other.

"They both have the same participant ID, the same date on the form, right?"

Danny nodded.

"The left hand photo was taken on August 17 at 10:23 AM according the date stamp on the file. The right hand photo, same subject id, same date as the other photo, was taken on October 24 at 4:20PM."

Stephen looked Danny in the eye and put his finger down on the left photo.

"In the photo that was taken in August, the CD4 value is 850 which is getting low so it triggered an automatic red letter 'Q' next to that number. See?" Danny looked at the red 'Q' icon next to the number 850 and nodded.

Stephen jabbed his finger down on the right hand photo.

"In this photo of the same CRF taken two months later in October, the CD4 count is now 1,135 which is not abnormal."

Danny said, "So what? Someone changed the data."

"But look!" Stephen gave Danny more of '*The Professor*'.

"Do you see the white flag next to the 1,135?" He pointed to the October photo again.

The white flag was clearly visible against the light blue background of the web page.

Danny was forced to nod again.

"That white flag means that no one has ever changed the data – there is no audit trail because the data never changed. That is the bedrock of the EDC system – when someone changes case report form data in the EDC system, the flag next to the data changes color from white to blue – an audit trail of data changes is automatically, inviolably kept by the EDC system.

"These two photos show that the data *was* changed between August and October, but the October photo says that the query never existed and that even though the lab data changed from 850 to 1,135, it shows that according to the audit trail, the data never changed."

Danny resisted the urge to nod.

Danny said, "OK, even if you are sure that this happened, why is that so bad? Can't someone do something wrong and then this could happen?" he trailed off pointing to the printouts. "I mean, look at the Obamacare roll-out."

Stephen shook his head no said in a gravelly voice, "No, someone 'can't do something wrong' and make this happen."

Danny still only looked half convinced. Stephen said, "OK, I'll prove it. Look, let's log on to the AMP website and see what it says about auditing."

They browsed around AMP's website looking for descriptions of the EDC system. They quickly found the EDC PowerPoint presentation and they ran the slideshow until it got to the data security slides. Stephen went back and forth between two slides describing the colors of the flags related to data queries and the audit trail.

All data changes are fully recorded, the presentation said. Look at the flag colors, the presentation said. Trust us, the presentation said.

Stephen said, "Look, it's getting late. I'll take these printouts home and double check everything."

Chapter 28 – January 20

At 9PM, Danny got a series of urgent text messages from his Internet snooping program telling him that the DFS server needed to be rebooted - as soon as possible. That had happened two times over the last three days and they had both been false alarms. But Danny still wanted to deal with it before Ted saw it the next morning. The temperature had plummeted to 20 degrees with a strong cold breeze, so it wasn't his first plan for a pleasant evening.

Danny got into his Spider and drove to school in the frigid cold of the January night. He parked outside his office and rushed into the building, taking two steps at a time. Sitting in the server room, he quickly rebooted the server and sat back to wait the few minutes it would take.

Once the server was up and running again, Danny double checked it by sending an email to himself using his phone.

The email arrived in the school mail box almost automatically and no warning emails came from the Internet software. Apparently, the reboot fixed the problem. Danny reviewed the logs for the past few hours to see what could have caused the problem, but nothing jumped out at him. His knee bumped the lipstick USB drive which was still connected to the computer. He cursed under his breath and blamed his dad, but he didn't want to mess with it now.

Danny turned off the light in his office and headed back to his car in the cold. Twenty minutes tops, just like he had hoped.

The car started on the third try. The heater was just barely working. Danny turned left from the school onto the windy road that lead to highway 54. He was hungry and was thinking of stopping at the Indian place on the way home. But halfway down the huge hill, his car sputtered and died. Danny sneaked a look at the dashboard displays. He put the car in neutral and leaned on the brake to keep the car out of the tree lined ditch. The brakes were barely responsive but finally stopped the car at the bottom of the hill. The car was out of gas. No way, he thought. But he couldn't exactly remember the last time he filled the tank.

He took out his phone and called his dad.

"Dad, my car ran out of gas about a mile from school on

Erwin Rd. Can you bring me a gallon or two to get me going?"

"I was definitely right about those SAEs, Danny. Somebody was hiding data that was going to stop the study." Stephen's excited voice ignored Danny's question.

"Dad, it's cold so I'm going to wait in the car. Can you come now?"

"Didn't you hear me? I know what that USB password means!"

"You already said. It was an anagram for those random letters on the USB note. By the way, you left the USB in the server at school."

"No," Stephen said. "I mean, yes, it's an anagram, but it's really two anagrams!"

"What?" Danny could barely take the one anagram theory.

"Danny, the second anagram is 'He is hiding SAEs'. I don't know who 'he' is, but I'm betting it's someone on the trial at AMP. Alexandria Knott didn't think those changing lab data points was a mistake, she knew someone did it on purpose to hide SAEs. I'll come pick you up and then we'll call Detective Roberts. And be careful waiting on that road, it's dark. I'll be there in fifteen minutes."

Finally. "OK, I'll be waiting." Danny ended the call. He turned the lights off and pushed the car was as far off the road as he could without getting stuck in the mud. Even though it was cold, he changed his mind and waited outside the car. The full moon crested the pitch black tree line. He leaned against the hood and used his iPhone to look up 'anagram' to make sure he knew exactly what it meant.

He looked up from his phone whenever a car came down the hill, each time hoping it was his father. After a few minutes of no cars passing, a white car came over the hill and sped towards Danny. The car seemed to be headed along the edge of the road, coming right towards him.

I can smell the water, it's this way, the doe thought. She cocked her ear and heard her baby buck across the road. She heard the sound of The Others, the loud sound that didn't even try to conceal itself but was still dangerous. She turned around and saw the young buck about to enter the street. She leapt over the hard ground in the clearing of the trees to stop him.

The car was accelerating towards him. Danny froze and couldn't decide whether to jump onto the hood of his car or into the woods or to run across the street. The full moon shone onto the driver and Danny saw a familiar face and bald head. It was Arthur Moore and he looked determined to run Danny over.

Danny was about to dive into the woods when a large deer jumped into the road and stopped in between him and the car. The deer was frozen in the headlights. The car tried to swerve, but there was no time.

The car hit the deer.

My baby buck.....

The deer slid up the hood and into the windshield.

It wasn't supposed to be this way, Arthur thought during the last second of his life. I was trying to help people with my vaccine. Why did she have to break the rules and then threaten to make the SAE's public? I saw the problem and I was going to fix it, without ruining everything. I knew she had something on her phone in that meeting – the way she looked at it when asked if she had evidence. When she left her phone in the conference room, I saw my opportunity to clone her phone and see what she had. I had Blake paged to get him out of the conference room. Cloning her phone with Bluetooth was easy but when I looked at the clone later I was shocked - those pictures of the data screens on her phone, the as yet unsent memo describing the database problems. And the photos of her and that ice cream vendor I'd overheard at the baseball picnic.

When I saw that Christmas party invitation with that ice cream vendor on her phone, it all came to me at once. That almost made it seem right, like I was supposed to do it. I could get some cyanide from the lab after a lecture at State and I could poison the almond ice cream that she made especially for Knott. Almond flavored cyanide in almond flavored ice cream - perfect! My theater training was still intact enough that I could put on a wig and makeup and play a waiter at the Christmas party. The dose was enough to knock her off the trial for a while, but probably not enough to kill her.

That would have given me time to fix the formulation and save the company.

And then this kid at that school was poking around my web site, looking at the description of the EDC audit trail and query features. When I snooped on his server and saw that he had the photos on a USB drive – still connected to the server – I just had to do something. I lured him to the school a few times with those bogus emails that looked like they were sent by his Internet snooping program but I didn't really have a plan. Then when I saw how old his car was, I figured that no one would suspect cut brake lines – that car was a piece of junk. If the cut brake lines didn't do the job then I would finish him of here on the road. For good measure, I drained his gas tank. When he drove off, I broke into the school and took that USB from the server. After that, I followed his followed his usual path and saw him walking on the road right in front of me. It was like I was supposed to do it again.

The deer went through the windshield and into the driver.

The car veered to the right and slammed into a tree less than fifty feet from Danny.

Danny stood shocked for a full minute and then walked slowly over to the smoldering car, stunned at nearly having died but obligated to look into the smoking wreck. The deer was lodged in the windshield and Arthur Moore. Both were clearly dead. The smoke drove Danny back a few steps. He called 911 and then put his hands in his pockets and walked back to his car to wait for his father and the police.

Chapter 29 – January 28

Danny was at his father's house and Stephen was reading the newspaper article and summarizing out loud to Danny.

"First, the good news: Alexandria Knott is recovering and will be discharged from the hospital sometime next week."

Stephen adjusted the paper, squinted through his reading glasses, and read in his newsman voice.

"The newspaper is all over this story. High tech and sex. Let's see…. The police say he poisoned Knott because she had evidence on her phone that showed he was hiding bad safety data. The phone also contained a memo detailing how safety data from the clinical trial was being erased for financial reasons.

"The police found a CD of a clone of Knott's phone in his office. Apparently, Knott's phone also had some photos of Alexandria Knott and Tammy Rose that indicated that they had a close personal relationship. From notes on a legal pad found with the CD, it was also apparent that Moore also somehow knew that Tammy always made a small batch of Alexandria's favorite flavor, almond ice cream. Knott's cloned phone also contained a meeting reminder on her Outlook calendar for the Ninth Street Merchants Association Christmas party. It showed the list of people RSVP'ing and catering, and he saw Tammy Rose's name on it. Arthur Moore was using all that to frame Tammy Rose, and it worked because she was arrested."

Stephen skimmed and then turned to the jump on page five.

"Moore put everything the company had behind his clinical trial. He was worried mostly about the venture capitalists and their financial analysts. Moore knew that if any serious adverse event reports became public before he could fix them, that would stall the trial and that would kill his company."

Stephen stopped and put the paper down.

"When will they get to the part where I figured it out?" Stephen asked Danny.

Stephen looked for his place again in the article.

"Moore decided that he could infiltrate the waiter staff at the party; his theatre training in college paid off. They found the costume and wig in his house. After Tammy Rose arrived with her ice cream deserts, he then just stirred the powdered arsenic into the ice cream container labeled 'A' for Alexandria. He passed out the ice cream in his 'shaggy wig' waiter disguise."

"I remember him," Danny said shaking his head.

Stephen put down the newspaper, stood up, and stretched his right leg.

"The police never found Knott's phone at the Christmas party but they assume Moore took it in the confusion after he poisoned her. Danny, once you started visiting AMPs website from the Durham Friends School server, Moore's snooping programs started tracking you. When we were looking at the lipstick/USB computer screen photos on the DFS server, Moore was tracking our actions with *his* snooping program. He could also tell that the USB drive was still connected to the server.

"It says here" Stephen sat down and picked up the newspaper again "that Detective Lewis Roberts was already investing Alexandria Knott's work colleagues and would have gotten around to Arthur Moore eventually."

Stephen went to the kitchen and opened two more 1554 beers, stretching his bad knee in the process. He gave one to Danny and then sat down again.

"After seeing those photos first on Knott's phone and then on the USB attached to your server, Moore was desperate to get you out of commission, for at least a while. Moore had hacked into the snooping program you had running, Danny... sorry about that – he was a little bit better at computers than I am. Moore had your snooping system send you emails saying that the DFS system was under attack and that would lure you to the school. When you went in to check the server, he sabotaged your car. When you drove off, he broke into the server room and took the USB drive in the server. Sorry about that, too, that was my fault, I should have taken the USB with me. He had the USB drive on him after the accident."

Stephen put the paper down and stared jokingly at Danny.

"That clown thought that you were the one who knew what was going on. He was going after the wrong guy." Danny thought he heard an odd tone is his dad's voice but when he looked over to him, the newspaper was up again and Stephen was reading.

"It says here that Blake Roth has been given temporary control of company by the board and says that he is planning to test the new formulation that Moore had been planning. Let's see.....There is a rumor that 90% of the company had been leveraged to the venture capitalists as the price for keeping the company alive during this trial. Roth is quoted as saying that the clinical trial can still show that AMP's HIV vaccine will be effective. It says that they are not sure if the venture capital company will stop funding the line of research or not."

Danny stood up, glad to have the episode behind him.

"Hey, Dad, by the way, how did that junk email/art project end up?"

Stephen looked up to Danny with a huge smile on his face.

"It won an award at the user's group annual meeting. The judge said, and I quote, it's *rare* that you see this *medium* so *well done*."

Epilogue - February 4

Alexandria was sitting at home in an overstuffed chair, in her robe, drinking tea, looking out the window during the February rain. She closed her eyes and imagined again that the background drone of the I-40 traffic was really the low roar of a North Carolina mountain waterfall.

Her phone rang. Her landline – she hadn't replaced her cell phone since she came out of the hospital. She leaned to pick it up and grimaced with the residual pain of her poisoning. On the second try she picked up the phone.

"Hello?"

After a short pause, a voice said "Can I come over?"

She smiled and listened to the voice inside. "Sure, I was hoping it was you."

ABOUT THE AUTHOR

Patrick Murphy is a clinical trial data manager in Research Triangle Park, North Carolina. He lives on a farm in Durham, North Carolina. He holds a bachelor of science degree in Chemical Engineering from Northwestern University.

36139347R00112

Made in the USA
Lexington, KY
07 October 2014